Death of a Mermaid

Diane needed to cut away the chaff and expose the heart of the Mermaid Nerissa case. Her questions piled up fast. Did the mermaid die because of threatened power? Could be. Did the mermaid die because of jealousy? Perhaps. Did she die because of money? Hardly. So then, did the mermaid die because of politics? Hmm.

Or, did Nerissa die because of something she knew that she shouldn't have? No indication of that. Did the mermaid die because of secret sex? Unlikely, Diane figured. If those questions about motive weren't enough, WHO did it, what was the murder weapon, and what happened to it?

Fighting discouragement, Diane went back inside. She'd devoted herself to making a difference in people's lives by ridding society of low-life trouble. But maybe she wasn't cut out for this line of work after all. The errant thought was too painful to entertain. If Tom knew, he would calmly say, "Nobody ever said this was easy. Get back to work, dear, and we'll celebrate when you've solved the case. And I *know* you will."

Table of Contents

What They Are Saying About Death of a Mermaid
Death of a Mermaid
Acknowledgements
Dedication.
Prologue 1
Chapters 6
    One 6
    Two 13
    Three 20
    Four 26
    Five 33
    Six 42
    Seven 50
    Eight 57
    Nine 64
    Ten 69
    Eleven 78
    Twelve 85
    Thirteen 91
    Fourteen 94
    Fifteen 98
    Sixteen 105
    Seventeen 114
    Eighteen 120
    Nineteen 126
    Twenty 130
    Twenty-one 137
    Twenty-two 143
    Twenty-three 149
    Twenty-four 157
Meet Karen Hudgins.
Other Works From The Pen Of Karen Hudgins.
Visit Our Website

What They Are Saying About Death of a Mermaid

Oh, my goodness! This story is a delight. It kept me interested, engrossed, and obsessively turning to the next page. Karen has made magic happen here.
—Em Jacobs, Reader

Death of a Mermaid is a delightful mystery. A witty, clever "tail" that I thoroughly enjoyed!
—Carrie Graham, Blogger

Karen's *Death of a Mermaid* is engrossing and beautifully written. It's gripping and suspenseful all the way to the end!
—Darla Hower Mader, Reader

Death of a Mermaid

Karen Hudgins

A Wings ePress, Inc.
Mystery Novel

Wings ePress, Inc.

Edited by: Rebecca Smith
Copy Edited by: Jeanne Smith
Executive Editor: Jeanne Smith
Cover Artist: Syneca Featherstone

All rights reserved

Names, characters and incidents depicted in this book are products of the author's imagination or are used fictitiously. Any resemblance to actual events, locales, organizations, or persons, living or dead, is entirely coincidental and beyond the intent of the author or the publisher.

No part of this book may be reproduced or transmitted in any form or by any means, electronic or mechanical, including photocopying, recording, or by any information storage and retrieval system, without permission in writing from the publisher.

Wings ePress Books
www.wingsepress.com

Copyright © 2019 by: Karen Hudgins
ISBN 978-1-61309-594-2

Published In the United States Of America

Wings ePress Inc.
3000 N. Rock Road
Newton, KS 67114

Acknowledgements

My forever thanks go to my beta readers and writer friends at Pen Drop Coffee Break, Colorado Springs, CO. During our weekly meetings, many of you have helped me create this book through sharing our passion for writing, expertise, striving for excellence, and kind support. So glad I found you! Thanks also to George Papcun for his suggestions that led me to try new things. Last, but hardly least, my heartfelt thanks to my editor, Jeanne Smith, who never fails to give my work her best.

Dedication

For Jax Hawkins, keep loving life's mysteries, Grandma.
Writer friend Gloria "Glo" Ferguson, ever-comforting.
Writer friend Pegeen Brent, often inspiring.

Prologue

Blue Wave Resort
Ponte Vedra Beach, FL

Chelsea Graham, a.k.a. Mermaid Nerissa, wrapped her hand around the driftwood door handle to Neptune's Grotto and pulled. The door wouldn't budge. Apparently, the maintenance men hadn't re-adjusted the hinges, leaving a fifty-fifty chance of getting one side to open. She frowned at the inconvenience and knocked on the dark glass. Her appointment might already be inside. Yet, no one answered.

Putting more oomph into it, she tugged again—and nothing happened. She considered entering the posh water theater where she worked through the back way, but a co-worker passed by and said, "Hey, d'you need some help with that?"

Chelsea nodded and stepped aside. Luckily, the bartender had the right touch, and one of the double portals swung open. Giving him a high-five, she said, "Thanks," and walked into the hushed, dim showroom.

Glancing around, she did indeed find herself alone. She soaked up the quiet and space. Her last appearance about an hour ago had left her tired, happy, and secretly bittersweet. Everything had gone almost perfectly. She and the cast had earned a standing ovation. Only Sam, the ever-so-clever choreographer, would have caught the skipped beat in her final triple twist and flip sequence. Maybe even her Merman Triton co-star had noticed?

She prayed neither of them would call her on it. Then she'd have to come up with a lie about why she'd hesitated. No way could she reveal the reason.

She clutched the beach wrap that covered her red bathing suit. Her last-minute appointment was late. Some nerve, showing up late for a talk that they'd requested. Except it was partly understandable. So much was going on tonight for this year's Summer Splash Bash. Thousands of dollars were raised for autistic kids in Florida. Good feelings rose in the hearts of all involved, along with relief when it was over.

Thirst was getting the better of her. She ambled over to the bar, plucked a free bottled water from a large ice bucket and drank. Performing in three shows back-to-back this evening had even worn Chelsea out, and she was a veteran ballet swimmer. She could barely lift her sixty-pound silicone mermaid tail after the show, but her spent energy was worth it. All of her stringent training had paid off. She was on top of her game. Moreover, she got to do what she loved every day. Few could say that.

Then there was the fame that went with it. Tonight the Grotto had been packed with guests, and her Grandma Kitty had been in the audience. Sometimes, Chelsea and the others were given a bonus to split among them; a sweet gift from Apollo, the owner. Tonight had been one of those times. The extra cash would come in handy. Especially now.

Half smiling, she set the nearly empty bottle aside and stepped further into the spacious room. She focused on the water show tank that stretched from left to right in front of banks of tables. She absolutely loved it. Wavy blue reflections rippled out into the room. They drifted lazily over her and the tables. The hum of the filtering system could be heard if one listened closely enough.

The aquarium was a contemporary technological wonder. For Chelsea, it was her professional office. She walked to the polished, thick glass front and fondly laid her hand on the cool surface. Oh, how realistic everything looked from out here. Acrylic seaweed swayed in front of her and five kinds of coral hid air tubes. The giant pearly clamshell sat in the center, ready to open or close on cue.

Chelsea sighed, knowing she'd lucked out with landing this gig. Being a mermaid was an unusual vocation. She'd taken it to the depths and back. But in this moment, sadness and pride filled her heart. Her glorious career would soon end. For now, only she knew.

"Goodbye," she murmured to the aquarium, as if to a best friend.

Chelsea turned away from the tank and walked to the edge of a table in the first row of seating. Time was fleeting. Guests were expecting her to return to the Post-Show Party at the pool outside on the second terrace. She wrapped her arms around herself and looked down at the thick carpet under her flip flops. Its wavy design was an original and expensive, like many other features there. Yet, amidst all this extravagance, something was missing.

Him. Her love, Luke. She was so disappointed with his message:

Babe, I won't be there tonight. Got a last minute dive charter. He's paying double, and I'll be out for two days. I'm sorry. I love you.

She longed for his hugs, his praise. Still, she'd understood how work came first in their lives. Looking back, she'd often foregone fun times for hours of practice in pools, studios, and gyms. Somehow, though, when Luke had come along, she'd made time for him, as he had done for her. Tonight was special—a showcase of quality in her work world. But she'd have to wait to bask in his admiration again.

Crossing her arms, Chelsea shifted her weight from one foot to the other. With Apollo's water shows, there was no seven-minute delay for late-comers. So, she'd honed a habit for punctuality. Now she hated being late. She'd give this another three minutes, then leave.

She eyed the smoky glass front doors, barely able to see through them. Only shadows passing. Suddenly, she sensed the warmth radiating from someone standing close behind her. She stiffened. Her breath caught in her throat as she was roughly grabbed.

The intruder encircled her upper body with an arm and tightened just below her neck. Chelsea shrieked in surprise and strained forward. She tried to turn and face her attacker, but to no avail.

Losing her balance, she arched her back. Shock rearranged her senses. Her strength wavered. Her intuition spiked. Whoever it was they meant business. Intentional evil business. When she'd said goodbye moments earlier, she hadn't meant like this!

The dimmed lights, tables, the reflections—even the bar with its towers of shiny glasses—all smeared together in a sweep from her widening eyes. During her outraged cry came the first blow. A sharp, irregular tool tore into her neck with a vengeance.

Burning and tearing muscle and flesh, the weapon was stealing her life as hot blood spurted over her collarbones. It coated her skin and splashed down her forearms. Tears sprang forth. Her heart thumped into a deafening frenzy.

The next blow ripped open her right carotid artery. Gurgles of protest escaped her throat as her knees buckled. Nausea took over. Her scattered mind somehow cried, *Help! Please help me!*

Finished, her attacker released the death grip and allowed her to slump to the floor. Warm, blood-soaked carpet cushioned her cheek. The odor repulsed her, and she caught a familiar whiff of mint.

Why? Oh, why? died on her lips.

In her final, broken breath, Mermaid Nerissa looked into the blue-green water where she'd spent so many happy hours. Her gaze landed on her favorite coral with its round pink crown. Raising a shaky forefinger, she jabbed at the glass and stared at the red streak she was leaving behind in the wake of her death.

Chapters

One

There's a New P.I. in Town

Atlantic Beach, Florida
Almost a year later

Diane Phipps, P.I., raised her eyes from scouring the old news clippings. Frowning at the palm trees swaying outside her office window, she wrestled with the question that wouldn't go away, "Who'd want to murder a mermaid?"

Her words hung in the morning air like a sleepless ghost. Fretting aloud made her query weigh more. The silence that followed magnified it, taunting Diane's crime-solving spirit and sharpening her impetus to find out.

Despite sheriffs' detectives working the homicide since last July, the case remained unsolved. It tainted the lives of people close to the victim, Chelsea Graham. Known as "Mermaid Nerissa" at the posh Blue Wave Resort, she'd lost her bright future—without someone to hold accountable.

With pastel sky colors, low puffy clouds, and soft air sweeping the strife of life out to sea, this beachside paradise seemed an unlikely place for such ugliness. But Diane's new neighbor, Kitty Swan, Chelsea's grandmother, could confirm this kind of heartache existed.

"She's in my heart every day," Kitty often cried out.

Widowed and a retired reference librarian, Kitty still had no closure from Chelsea's death. The memorial service had come and gone, but Kitty needed answers to move on.

Diane understood. Her new friend echoed the reason for seeking justice. Here, Diane could help for the sake of safer society and as a favor to Kitty. Her welcome had rung true when Diane and Tom had arrived in Marsh Point and rented a bungalow along the Intracoastal Waterway in Northeast Florida. When Diane needed an office, a tip from Kitty led her to leasing this one-story, wood-framed cottage in Atlantic Beach.

Diane paid little mind to how its sea green front door and weathered shutters needed new paint. Having a space to call her own would help her level the scales between good and evil. Evil had certainly roared, paid a visit to Chelsea, and taken its toll.

At 9 a.m. on Thursday, Kitty's knock on the front door brought Diane's gaze back to her desk. She stuffed the news clippings into an expanding folder and rose from the old roller chair. She swiped at her chestnut brown hair and straightened the light cotton slacks she'd only unpacked yesterday.

She crossed the space, which was double what she'd had above the leather shop in St. Louis. Tom's new surveillance career move had brought inconveniences—and some perks. Diane having this ground-floor office was one. After passing through the small foyer, she opened the door and greeted her first official client.

"Hello, again," Diane said warmly.

Kitty stepped inside, gave her a brief hug, and fanned her face with her fingers.

"My, oh my, it's already getting warm. But I hear rain's on the way, not that it'll make much difference." In her fifties, she stood taller than Diane's five foot six inches. Kitty's blue linen shirt complimented her sapphire eyes. Her printed skirt covered her calves. Shoulder-length gray hair brushed against her high, pinkish cheekbones. A smart leather purse hung from her shoulder.

"C'mon in," Diane said, smiling. "I hope you didn't have trouble parking."

Kitty issued half a smile. "It's still early, so finding a space is easier."

Diane led Kitty past a side room and a little kitchen as they entered what was once a living room. Rectangular, with small windows along one side and at the far end, the space was a work-in-progress. It gave Diane a viable start with a credible address.

Kitty's eyes sparkled softly. "This is nice. I love wood floors."

"Me, too," Diane agreed, despite how those needed refinishing, "And lots of windows." Her desk, an old fashioned file cabinet, and a work table nearly filled the far end. "I couldn't have found this without your putting me in touch with the owner. Here, have a seat."

Diane gestured toward the yellow floral chintz chair she'd brought from her former office. Favorite treasures like this couldn't be left behind when she and Tom had moved.

"Would you like some iced tea?"

"Sweet, please." Kitty settled in the chair and crossed her legs at her ankles. Her rosy lipstick was still bright. Turned down at the corners, her mouth gave the impression she was irritable. She sat more primly than in her home kitchen last week when she had first told Diane about the horrific tragedy with her granddaughter Chelsea.

Diane handed her a glass of tea and a napkin with flamingos on it. She rounded the end of her desk and took her seat. "How're you holding up?" she asked, as some days were better than others for Kitty.

Kitty finished her first sips and dabbed her lips with the napkin. She still seemed a bit proper to Diane, but her gentleness made up for it. "I'm better, because you're helping me with this." Unabashed hope filled her eyes, which fed Diane's determination.

"When you'd confided in me, it struck a nerve," Diane said. "Crime always does that to me. I can't let these things pass without getting to the bottom of what happened. I'll do my best, and we'll see what comes of it."

Relief crossed Kitty's face.

"With no fee," Diane added. "I owe you."

Kitty met her gaze. "I'll not be able to thank you enough." She paused and said, "I've gone through Chelsea's things again in the guest room and have found nothing unusual. But I brought this along. It's a picture of her and her boyfriend, Luke Talbot." She pulled the item from her bag, slid her fingers along the bamboo frame, and handed it over the desk to Diane.

Diane titled her head to one side. "Lovely couple, and he looks like a nice guy." His ruffled, dark hair fringed his forehead. His smile could melt an ice block. He was bare-chested, wore diving gear, and held a mask in his hand.

Kitty shrugged slightly and her chin quivered. "I guess so."

Diane hiked an eyebrow. "Do you have doubts?"

"Nothing in particular to dislike about Luke, but since someone killed my granddaughter I really don't know who's nice and who isn't. Still, Chelsea never complained about him, and he was inconsolable at her funeral."

Diane nodded. "Losing a loved one, no matter how young or old, is traumatic."

Her insides tightened as she lowered her gaze to the picture in her hand. *Not now*, she told herself. *Not the time for me to reminisce about losing Dad.* She set the photo aside and scribbled a new note on the pad in front of her.

Kitty pulled a tissue from her bag. "The suddenness of it all still shakes me."

Diane set down the pen. She'd gone over everything Kitty had first told her and had begun filling out a customized form she'd created for her cases. She preferred to initially write them by hand. Somehow, it made her job feel more personal. *Personal* held a sort of power that helped her dig deeper for answers. Eventually, she would transcribe it all into a computer file to go over later, often into the night.

So far, Chelsea's case was a homicide that stood a chance of going cold. Budget and staff cuts were unraveling the local sheriff's office. Hopefully, Diane's presence, her fresh dark eyes and persistence, would turn up something new to help build a strong case against the perp that would stick in court.

Diane cleared her throat. "It's not going to be easy."

"I expect so."

"Right."

They never are. Diane wanted to stress this. But Kitty needed encouragement.

"In review, here's what I have at the moment." She tapped the file folder. "Bear with me. It's cut and dried: We have a body. We know when and where the murder was committed. People of interest were interviewed, but no prime suspect has emerged. No witnesses. Nothing unusual left in her e-mails, voice mails, or text messages. No one has been charged with the crime." She rested her chin on the heel of her hand. "Oh, and the murder weapon is still in question and missing."

Kitty sniffled into a tissue, while Diane fidgeted inside. The last item dropped a red flag into her lap. A visit with the medical examiner might help her beyond "a sharp, irregularly-shaped object possibly barbed." Reaching final, air-tight conclusions on any case could be difficult on a good day. Without the weapon, the local DA could still decide to charge a suspect if he chose to do so. Not conclusive enough to satisfy Diane, though. In the end, an innocent suspect could go up the river, or a jury could set a murderer free.

Diane wiggled her foot with annoyance. She was out to do this right with no ambiguous, messy, unjust outcomes. Idealistic as it seemed, she adored orderliness in her kitchen at home *and* in her cases. Securing proof beyond shadow of a doubt about whodunit, why and how, drove Diane to the finish line and most judges to throw the book at a suspect.

Kitty's cell phone rang and she jumped. She pulled it from her purse and checked the screen. "I'm sorry. It's the vet. My cat's having surgery, and they're calling me with a report."

Diane nodded. "Sure, take your time."

While Kitty attended to her call, Diane quickly left her desk and went to the kitchen for a plate of pecan mini-rolls. While they warmed in the microwave, this new case roiled in her mind. It was already picking up momentum.

Yesterday she'd stopped by the local sheriff's office, provided her credentials, and met Detective Beau Brooks. He'd worked on Chelsea's case before being pulled off for a recent homicide attempt against a well-known local shrimper.

She'd learned that Detective Brooks' follow-up on Chelsea's case was reduced to sporadic. He had a boss to keep happy. Diane fretted over this, but she didn't rock the boat with him. She would rather gain a reputation for solving crimes, not being a meddling pain.

By the end of their meeting, Detective Brooks had taken Diane further into his confidence. He'd shared some of Chelsea's case files, and she accepted his stale coffee offer. It had been a stimulating joining of like minds devoted to finding truth. Almost fun, *except* it was about something awful.

Investigating homicide was never fun. Yet Chelsea's job of being a professional mermaid *shouted fun.* She'd been a rising star and had ridden high waves of success…until someone had snuffed out her life last July. Determined, Diane plunged in head-first to find out who had done the dreadful snuffing.

Two

Chelsea and That Night

When Diane returned with the rolls, Kitty was putting away her phone.

"How's your cat?" Diane asked.

Kitty's expression brightened. "Arthur has to stay for another day, but he's okay."

Diane gave silent thanks because Kitty had enough turmoil to handle without losing her cat. Coming here this morning to talk about Chelsea was trying enough. It all had started when Kitty had invited Diane for coffee, and Diane had noticed a photo of Mermaid Nerissa in Kitty's kitchen. Naturally, Diane's curiosity flared. Kitty had opened up about what had happened to her beloved granddaughter.

That night Diane had told Tom about it, and he'd advised her to go for it. She was grateful for that. His support came more easily now. For a long while, though, Tom was reticent about her striking out on her own to solve crimes. Back in St. Louis, he'd preferred she'd stayed with the force downtown.

Then, when Diane had gone solo, she'd intrepidly solved her first case—the baffling Thurman Cole case. That had put her name on the P.I. map, and Tom had endearingly conceded that she'd found her niche. The nameplate resting front and center on her desk was a gift from him. It was the first thing she had unpacked from boxes labeled 'Diane's Office.'

Diane offered Kitty a cinnamon roll, resettled herself at her desk, and reviewed her note pad.

"So, let's pick up again. You said Chelsea didn't complain about Luke, but did she complain about anybody else?"

Kitty brushed a pecan crumb from the corner of her mouth. "Not to me. But you know how it is with boyfriends and girlfriends. They share almost everything, so maybe Luke would know better than me." She took another bite of the mini-roll. "My, these are good."

"Tom made them." She already missed him. He'd only been gone one day.

"Well, there was a while when Chelsea was troubled about work."

Diane gazed at her with keen interest. "Troubled? Did she share about what or why?"

Kitty shook her head back and forth. "No. Although, one evening she'd come to dinner. I'd made her favorite shrimp pasta, but she seemed preoccupied. When I'd asked if she was okay, she'd said something had come up about her work."

"What was it?"

"Nothing she wanted to talk about." Kitty slowed for a breath. "So I didn't pry."

Diane jotted and Kitty went on.

"Chelsea was mostly a happy woman. Twenty-six, mind you, with a bright future. She was very good at being a mermaid. She had brains, too. She'd earned a degree in marine biology with honors and supported sea life protection. She earned a sound salary and made special appearances at private parties, once even in Los Angeles."

Diane leaned forward. "I wish I could've met her and seen her perform."

Kitty twisted the tissue in her hand. "You would've been impressed. Water ballet and marine life always appealed to her. Her soul got all wrapped up in them. In that way, she took after my mother, who was Chelsea's great-grandmother Sophia."

Diane washed down her next bite of pastry with a sip of tea. "How so?"

"Nana loved water shows, and there wasn't an Esther Williams movie she hadn't seen."

Diane had only seen clips, and she'd found them entertaining. "Your granddaughter was lucky to find work she loved."

"Lots don't," Kitty humphed. "But I loved my library work, too. I'd helped people know more." Kitty moved the plate to the chair arm. "When the police talked with me, I tried to help them as much as possible. They came twice to see me. Chelsea's parents live in Fort Myers on the Gulf side. They own a bed and breakfast. They almost wore out the roads right after she died. I've called the detective on the case often for updates. Chelsea was my only grandchild."

Diane's laptop dinged with a new email. She reached over and closed the lid. "This might be hard, but can we go back to that night when she died? Tell me again what you remember?"

Kitty nodded slowly. "To think I almost didn't go. My good friend June had caught a cold and couldn't go with me. But I went by myself. The event really was lovely…lovely."

Diane had heard of Blue Wave Resort, located further south along historic A1A in Ponte Vedra Beach.

"It does sound special. Upscale?"

"Quite so," Kitty assured. "The Summer Splash Bash is very popular and raises funds for fighting birth defects, the latest defect caused by the Zika virus. The Blue Wave is owned by Apollo

Redstone and his wife Naomi. Apollo's quite a character, and he takes worthy causes seriously. That night there were food tastings, music, and three special water shows in Neptune's Grotto. That's the dinner theatre where the shows happen."

"And Chelsea performed that evening?"

Kitty's eyes lit up. "Oh my, yes. Our Mermaid Nerissa stole the show. Not long after she started working for Apollo, he'd made her the star. Apollo's promotion of the show still is spread far and wide. Over the weeks she kept getting better and better. Her grace and moves had mesmerized people. Their applause thundered, which roused other guests' curiosity. So people rarely left the resort without having seen her show."

From the way Kitty was moving her hands, Diane could imagine its beauty.

"The choreographer created encores for her, the merman, and the rest of the cast."

Diane smiled. "There's a merman?"

Kitty smiled back. "Glory be, yes. Owen Wagner played King Neptune's son. He would rescue Nerissa when she got trapped inside the big clam shell."

Diane's heart fluttered. "Aww, a hero. Sounds romantic."

"Owen has left Blue Wave, but he was a hero in real life, too," Kitty provided. "A couple of years ago, he saved Apollo's son from a riptide. Their picture was in the *Beach Weekly Times*. Owen's an ex-swimming coach and engaged to Ava, a model. She often sat in the audience."

So, there were still happy endings in this paradise ran through Diane's mind. Searching her memory, she said offhandedly, "Wasn't Triton King Neptune's son?"

"Triton, yes," Kitty repeated. "And even if he didn't exist in mythology, if Apollo wanted King Neptune to have a son in the water show, there would be a son in the water show." She hesitated. "According to Chelsea, nobody argued with Apollo. Not for long, anyway."

Diane wrote another action note and related rationale. *Meet Apollo Redstone.* Power often masterminded homicides.

"How did Chelsea and Merman Owen get along?"

"Famously." Kitty pursed her lips.

Find Owen Wagner flowed from Diane's pen. Co-stars with big egos could get close enough for murder.

"Really?"

"Yes, ma'am. They did, even though he was supposed to be somewhat moody. But she had a way with people, and her boyfriend Luke had taken it like a pro. He's a deep-sea diver and owns a dive shop in Jax Beach. He'd understood how things were for Chelsea on the job." Kitty polished off the pastry. "I believe the idea is to keep things bubbly and pleasant at work, and when the shift's over, everybody goes home to snuggle with who really matters. For her, it was Luke." She added in a wistful tone, "I think he would've married Chelsea."

Diane's heart gave a sympathetic thump as she wrote *Meet Luke Talbot.* Sex and attractions also often asserted themselves in murders. It was a long shot, but maybe things weren't as hunky-dory between them as Kitty thought.

"Okay, so that night you watched Chelsea perform in the underwater show, and—"

"I'd watched all of them. They'd run forty minutes each. There was one at seven o'clock, and eight. The last-call show was at nine." She smiled. "Chelsea wore a different top and tail in each of them."

"Sounds elaborate."

"Rosa Delacroix, the wardrobe mistress, is phenomenal. Apollo doesn't pinch pennies when it comes to flamboyance. And Chelsea always wore a small gold butterfly pin I'd given her for her first performance at Blue Wave. She called it her good-luck charm."

Diane wrote some more and looked up. "Then what happened? After the last show?"

Kitty's face contorted into a frown. "Well, that's…that's when it happened." She drew her shaky hand to her mouth.

Diane gave her moment.

Kitty raised her fingers to indicate she was okay. "Anyway, I mingled. That's what we do at these things. Chat, give praise, and promise a check. After the last show, I'd gone outdoors by the double-deck pool. It's on two levels and an amazing affair with palm trees and a Tiki bar in the middle of one of them. It took me a while to find Chelsea because there were hundreds of people and different terraces and whatnot. But then I caught a glimpse of her in the pool with friends or fans. She was so personable."

"Do you remember about what time you'd seen her?"

"Hmm, that was around ten-thirty, or so. She'd worn a red bathing suit and had braided her hair. I snapped a picture of her on my cell phone, but it was from a distance. She's almost lost in the crowd in that one." Kitty rubbed the handle of her purse with her thumb. "We were supposed to meet at eleven o'clock at the valet station in the front lobby. But…she never…came. I waited for her and figured she'd lost track of time. But by midnight, I was getting very tired and concerned. Chelsea was usually very punctual."

Diane slid her gaze to Luke's picture. "Was Luke there?"

She refastened her gaze on Diane. "No. Chelsea said he was called out to sea on a private diving excursion down the coast. She was disappointed about it. I'd offered to drop Chelsea off at her apartment at the end of the evening. That's why I was waiting for her. About the time I decided to go back out to the pool area to look for her, a firetruck and an ambulance drove up fast into the front driveway. The sirens wailed and the lights flashed. The EMTs had rushed into the lobby. There was such a commotion. I'd thought someone had an accident out at the pool. I never...*ever* expected it was all over my Chelsea."

Anguish echoed in Kitty's voice. She ran her fingertips over her mouth like a weaver's shuttlecock flying on a loom.

"Someone had found her?" Diane asked softly.

Kitty sighed heavily. "A maintenance worker had found her in Neptune's Grotto. I'd heard that he went in to fix a door or something. He called hotel security. When I heard people saying her name, I nearly fainted, I tell you. I told a medic who I was, and he had asked me to stand by. Humph! I didn't want to *stand by anywhere*. I only wanted to go to my granddaughter, tell her everything was going to be okay, to comfort her. Then, the police came, and..."

Three

Friends or Foes?

Diane regarded Kitty for a moment. The woman's frown lines deepened as she turned her head and gazed out the window. Fat raindrops pelted the panes. "Sometimes I still have to remind myself that she's gone."

Diane's disgust flared. The psychopath who had caused all this heartache was still on the loose. Her neighbor slowly pulled herself back to the moment. The more Diane could learn from her the better, and she pressed on.

"I need to ask...but with whom didn't Chelsea get along? I mean, we all usually run into a fly in the ointment."

Kitty turned back to her. "Like I told the detective, there was only one time when Chelsea mentioned a difficulty with a person, and that was with Hannah Hart. She was second mermaid, and I can't remember if it was over mermaid tails, the dressing room, or rehearsal times. But Hannah was raising a fuss. It all had fallen by the wayside soon enough, because they went to St. Augustine together to celebrate Hannah's birthday two days before Chelsea died."

More scribbling from Diane followed. *Meet Hannah Hart.* Money, fame, jealousy often asserted themselves in heinous crimes. She put down her pen and raised the blind to allow in more light.

Kitty stirred. "Do you miss St. Louis?"

Diane sat back. "At times, and I left some friends behind, like Emily."

"Hmm. Chelsea had a best friend, Jennifer McCall. They went to UF together. She's now a researcher at Cousteau Marine Labs and lives in Fort Caroline. This whole thing with Chelsea made her sick. Truly. We went to the cemetery together once, and she threw up in the grass."

Diane wrote *meet Jennifer*. Best friends either knew all or could stifle resentments leading to murder.

"Do you go often? To the cemetery?" she asked.

"Less than I used to," Kitty replied. "Sometimes I have company. Others came to pay their respects or just sit for a bit and talk as if she were there with them. I often feel that she's there when I visit. Visitors leave shells on her headstone, flowers, or a picture. Especially so right after this frightful thing happened. That's how I met Victor Chu and Eric Jameson. They work at Blue Wave. Victor is the bartender at the Tiki Bar, and Eric is the top chef. He also does the ice sculptures for big parties. He made an *amazing* one of King Neptune for Summer Splash Bash night. I have a picture of it, too." She thought. "I took a lot of pictures that night. I was going to make an album with them for Chelsea for Christmas."

Diane rolled her pen in her palm. "I'd like to see them, if you don't mind."

Kitty quickly offered, "I'll drop them off this evening, if that'd be convenient."

Diane slid her gaze to her desk clock. It lived next to her knitting basket where she hid Clarice, her pearl-handled, snub-nosed revolver. "That'll be just fine, Kitty. Thank you."

Pleased, Diane smiled inside. People's snappies often provided clues and even alibis. She would check out Kitty's batch after she had dinner with herself again. Tom was away for another four days on a classified surveillance mission.

Perhaps she should get a cat, although Tom preferred kids and dogs. But kids weren't part of the picture in their household, and probably wouldn't be. This was their shared deepest disappointment. Two miscarriages had crushed Diane's motherhood dream.

"Whatever I can do to help catch whoever killed my Chelsea, I will."

Diane dropped the pen and rose from her chair. She walked around the desk and gave Kitty a hug. By then, Diane wished for a walk out on Jacksonville Pier. The big sky, cloudy toward the north and clear toward the south, and the rhythmic surf cleared her head. People fished and even told her about their catches. She had an unimposing manner that made folks want to chat, which came in more than handy in her work.

This was a good thing. Her list was growing for interviews for finding Chelsea's murderer. Hopefully, the perp would loosen up and let something slip. One little thing could make a world of difference, if she were sharp enough to catch it.

"I think we've had enough for this morning," Diane told her. "Before you go, though, you've been living with this a lot longer than me. I'm wondering is there *anything* you have found curious about Chelsea's death?"

Kitty widened her eyes. "Why, there is one thing. Silly, I suppose, but I was surprised to find purple sequins from Chelsea's costume on Victor Chu's jacket lapel. Before all the commotion, I'd taken a photo of him and my friends Walter and Mimi Benning in front of the ice sculpture of King Neptune. Lots of people took pictures and selfies at that spot." She raised her hands to give an impression of its shape. "It looked like shimmering glass. Anyway, I hadn't looked at my photos for a long time."

"I can see why. Painful, I'm sure."

She nodded. "Well, I did a couple of weeks ago. It's funny how I hadn't noticed the sequins before. Then, they kind of popped out at me." She shook her head. "Those purple dots on Victor's lapel seemed out of place. So, I got out my magnifying glass to see them better. Sequins, I say! The same color as were on the costume top that Chelsea wore in her last show."

Diane involuntarily winced. "You have a very good eye, Kitty."

Kitty waved it off. "I used to do petit-point."

"Have you shared this sequin detail with Detective Brooks?"

Kitty frowned. "Detective Brooks is probably tired of me, and it takes him several days now to return my calls. So, no, I haven't shared it with him. Say, have you met him yet?" She again fanned her face with her fingers. "He's probably the most handsome man in the sheriff's office, you'll see."

Diane couldn't argue about that. Kitty also had a good eye for men. "Yes, we've met, and he knows I'm working 'informally' on this case. He's swamped, which is probably why he's slow to get back to you." She paused. "But this detail could be crucial."

Kitty pushed herself to her feet with some effort. "Oh, there's one more thing. The pin I'd given Chelsea went missing."

Another note hit Diane's page.

"Would seven be okay for you this evening?" Diane asked as she walked Kitty to the door.

"Perfect. I'll not miss it."

After they'd said their goodbyes, Diane returned to her desk and flipped through her note pages. Her mind churned over the situation. First, she'd never met a professional mermaid—alive, or dead. Chelsea wasn't the only mermaid at The Blue Wave, so Diane's odds of talking with these mythical swimmers rose on the horizon. Eager to visit the crime scene, she glanced at her calendar. Tomorrow was open. The sooner she drove down the coast to the resort, the better.

Another curious aspect tugged at her—apparently, no motive had surfaced. So, the reason *why* Chelsea was murdered was still hanging like a piñata full of facts waiting to be broken open. *Can I find its sweet spot?* zipped through her mind, bent on cracking this case.

Rolling her fingers on the desk surface, Diane hoped so. Her work was cut out for her. But nobody ever said detective work was easy, or else everyone would be doing it. Still, if Tom were here instead of being away, he'd say, "People can work hard at hiding things when they want to. They get good at it. So don't get discouraged if this takes a while."

Diane sat back in her chair. Well, Tom would surely know about that. It had taken years for his older brother to reveal his alcoholism, only to die from liver failure. And Diane knew about secretiveness, too. One of her lost loves had kept someone else's wife on the string for months. He'd worked hard at keeping that from her and everyone else...until discovered.

Diane figured Chelsea's murderer was working at it, as well.

"*Mistake, a big mistake,*" she said hotly.

Then another annoying detail was the missing and unconfirmed murder weapon. In general, disappearances piqued Diane's curiosity.

"People and things don't go poof!" she'd recently told Tom over coffee.

"Nope," he'd agreed. "The murderer ditched it, like most. But it's still up to us and the law to do our best to find them."

She had sighed. "Well, it certainly complicates things."

"Sometimes a disappearance *is* the case," he'd said thoughtfully. "*We* should look at it—"

"As a challenge."

"And as job security," he'd added wryly.

Challenge indeed. Chelsea had died from puncture wounds in her neck. What was used was unconfirmed by the medical examiner. So, who knew what to look for, or where?

Puzzled, Diane shook her head. Somehow, important elements had eluded Detective Beau Brooks. They had to be buried *deeply*, because aside from being built rock solid, he was 'smart as a whip,' as her mother would say. According to the detective and the records, a handful of persons of interest were interviewed, checked out, and let go.

"Nothing turned up from running the hotel registrations for guests with shady or criminal records or questionable connections to the victim," Detective Brooks had said. So it seemed unlikely a guest with a grudge had checked in with the motive to kill and then checked out with their mission accomplished.

Then, to clutter up the suspect possibility list, the Summer Bash Splash was open to the public. She wondered, too, if an attendee had come with murder on their mind? Or had a serial killer randomly picked the popular, beautiful Chelsea as his next target? Also, maybe someone had arranged for it to be done?

Those were all routes Diane yearned to explore. Haystacks hiding needles. She was dead sure, though, that perps screwed up more often than not. It would be up to her to open Pandora's Box and see what popped out.

Four

The Scene of the Crime

That night, Diane showered and dressed in her jammies. With luck, Tom would call. His current assignment kept him so incognito even she couldn't communicate with him. Kitty had come with her photos and gone. Diane had laid them in rows on the dining room table. She'd already been over them twice, and nothing unusual stood out to her. She turned out the chandelier light and trundled off to bed. Reviewing them in tomorrow's daylight could bring better results.

The phone woke Diane the next morning. A lot of static noise and wind came through.

"Tom? Is this you?"

"Hey, dear. I'm out at sea and only have a couple of minutes. But I love you, and how's the new case going?"

She rubbed her eyes. "I love you, too. The mermaid case is going to be a challenge. Nobody's got a real fix on it. When're you coming home?"

Tom spoke louder over the noise. "As soon as we catch this badass smuggler, and we're about to close in on him."

Smuggler? Intrigued, she pulled herself to the edge of the bed and let her feet dangle. Tom's work took him to all kinds of dirty deals, but this was a first. "So now you're in the smuggler catching business?" she half-joked.

"More like the diamond business for this go around. And you know it takes all kinds of scumbags in the world of crime. I'll fill you in when I get home. Probably next—"

A loud blast cut off the rest of his sentence. "Tom? Was that a gunshot? Tom!"

Dead silence hit her ear. She squeezed her eyes shut. Calling him back was out of the question. Danger had just erupted around him, and he used secured satellite lines while on deep remote duty. He was highly trained, and in moments like this, she could only rely on her trust of his uncanny, superlative skills. Her second best defense from emotional duress was throwing herself into her own current case. There was much to do for Mermaid Nerissa. Propelling herself into motion, she said goodbye to the silence, got up, and stretched.

Two hours later, Diane drove south on A1A on her way to the scene of the crime, Blue Wave Resort, for an informal walk-through. From Kitty's description, she expected a glitzy place Las Vegas style. Yet, as she pulled onto the steep stone driveway that led her up a hammock dune, she found the front of the resort quite understated. Instead of using valet service, she selected a space for parking her car and locked its doors.

The hotel was long and curved like a big S. The stylized contemporary name Blue Wave rolled over the front portico. Potted hibiscus and teak benches graced either side of the thick blue glass automatic doors with gold vertical pulls. Two bellmen, hair tinged blue, greeted her as she walked in.

Blown away by the lobby décor, she stopped in her tracks. Long chandeliers hung from the vaulted ceiling; island planters hugged peach walls where beach art was mounted. She skirted around a double-tiered fountain and crossed the pink marble floor at the registration desk.

Wearing crops, an artsy dolphin t-shirt, and sandals, Diane carried a straw bag and fit in with people casually coming and going. She got directions to Neptune's Grotto from a hostess who approached her. She headed down the hallway with its water-like lights playing on the walls and the low ceiling. Smooth charcoal gray stones stacked one atop the other formed a natural arch entrance over the smoky glass doors to the showcase water theatre.

There was a hush in the cool, spacious and partially dimmed room. The elaborate performance tank glowed. Coral, seaweed, and a large iridescent clamshell rested upon sparkly sand on the bottom. Diane paused and tried to believe that this was where people *worked*.

Alone, she walked to the front of the room and set her purse on a glossy black table. A soft whoosh and low hum from the glass tank was all she could hear while she oriented herself to what she remembered from the crime photos.

Crossing her arms, she stepped to the approximate spot where Chelsea lost her life. She looked down to where the floor met the low black base of the tank. The navy blue-edged carpet was immaculate and beautiful. No tangible proof, blood or otherwise, of Chelsea's existence remained.

"Excuse me?" came from behind her.

She jumped a bit and turned around. "Hello, I...I was just...admiring this room."

A large man with piercing dark eyes and thick, bushy hair took his hands out of his pockets and rocked back on his heels. "It *is* impressive, isn't it? We actually planned the rest of this wing of the hotel around this theater." He ambled toward her and halted at the table where her purse lay. "There isn't another like it around. No one else uses holograms underwater or creates bubbles big enough to swim into and out again." He tapped his finger against his temple and

Diane caught the initials AR monogramed on his shirt cuff. "That takes operative and creative genius, you see."

Diane cleared her throat. He certainly knew the details. "I do see, and you must be very proud of how it turned out."

The man eyed her for a moment and proffered his hand for a shake. "Have we met?"

"No, and I'm Diane Phipps."

"Apollo Redstone. This is my property. Have you seen one of our shows?"

Diane returned his shake and picked up her purse. "I've not had that pleasure yet, Mr. Redstone. But I do intend to catch some of them."

Apollo smiled and clapped his meaty hands together. "I don't think you'll be disappointed. Our concierge can help you with reservations." He gestured toward the door and waited for her to walk in front of him. "I hope to see you again soon."

Diane slowed her step and pulled a card from her pocket and gave it to him. "I'm wondering if you have a minute to talk."

He glanced down at the card. "You're a private investigator?" Surprise crossed his face.

She nodded. "I'm working on the Mermaid Nerissa case, and I think it'd be good for us to chat."

Redstone sobered. "The sheriff's detective and I have *chatted* often, Ms. Phipps. We've been trying to put the whole matter behind us around here. Having a murder occur in this famous site isn't good for business." He frowned. "I wish they could close this case."

"Yes. So do my client and others. I have a few questions."

The owner checked his watch. "If you make it brief, we can do it here. I've got to be upstairs in four minutes for a conference call." He raised a sudden finger. "And before we start I want to say that Chelsea was a major asset here, and our Blue Wave family misses her. You might want to stop at her memorial out on the back terrace. An eternal candle burns."

Diane moved closer. "That's kind of you." His concern seemed genuine. "May I ask how you met Chelsea?"

Apollo pulled out a chair for her. "Have a seat...my feet hurt."

She obliged and he sat opposite her. "I held auditions and she showed up late. But she had a good smile, nice hair and body, and she looked healthy. During her session she didn't use an air tube for almost six minutes, and our choreographer Sam Lock ranked her the highest in technical moves and ability to learn fast. I started her the next week. She didn't let us down once in the whole three years she performed here. I doubled her salary, promoted her to headliner, and advertised the hell out of her and the show. *That* was one of my better decisions."

Diane crossed her legs. "Was she grateful?"

Apollo crinkled his eyebrows. "She didn't kiss my ass, if that's what you want to know." He threw her a slight grin. "By the end, though, she was growing into a bit of an ingénue diva, got kind of cranky, and I only had to intercede once. But who cared? People came from around the state and Georgia to see her perform and spent money at Blue Wave. She did her job and got paid well."

Diane glanced at the tank. "Where were you when they found her?"

The CEO narrowed his eyes. "You mean, where was I when she was murdered?"

"That, too," she pressed. She needed to know and time was running short.

"You've got some guts, lady," he blurted. "But I can see you're trying to get to the bottom of this mess. So, *I* was in front of five hundred guests handing out comp tickets to raffle winners." He tapped his stubby forefinger on the table. "And *no way* would I get rid of the most popular and best of show revenue source my establishment has ever had. Think about it. I'm a businessman."

Diane was thinking about it. "Then Chelsea Graham was your favorite mermaid?"

Apollo dropped his voice. "She was, but don't let that get around. I've got two hundred and ten employees. Favorites cause dissention among the ranks."

Diane smiled. "Your secret's safe with me. There's one more thing, please. Did Chelsea ever confide in you…I mean, tell you something personal?"

Apollo tilted his head in thought. "Not really, but she had scheduled an appointment with me to meet the day after the Summer Splash Bash."

"Do you have any idea what about?"

He shrugged. "I'll never know, but I'd heard that she and Luke Talbot were secretly engaged. I expected she was going to ask for time off for a wedding." He touched the candle sitting in the middle of the table. "Shame, because we'd have thrown them a big celebration."

Diane blinked. *Chelsea was engaged?*

"That's what I heard from Owen Wagner," he offered. "He's Triton, the merman. He had a thing for her and kept an eye on her marital status."

Diane gathered her purse. "How do you suppose he found out?"

"Your guess is as good as mine. But since guesses don't count in murder investigations, maybe *you* should ask *him*?"

"Yes," she agreed, side-stepping his pointed tone. His patience with her impromptu visit was winding down.

"Time's up for me, Ms. Phipps. Make yourself at home. Look around all you like. The police scoured this place and didn't come up with anything. If our security cameras hadn't failed in zone eleven for fifty-seven minutes that night, we might be a lot further along."

"Zone eleven includes Neptune's Grotto?"

He nodded. "Inside and out on this end of the east-west corridor. It'd been giving us trouble last summer and was replaced after it cut out three times in different areas. Anyway, I hope you'll have better luck than the homicide team."

"Thank you, Mr. Redstone, and I do appreciate you spending time with me."

Apollo rose from the chair, and Diane followed him through the door and entered the wide hall. He bid her goodbye as she turned away and blended in with the other guests making their way to various resort venues. She passed the hairdresser, a surf shop, and the jewelry store featuring shells entwined with gold wire. Signage soon led her to her next stop: Pelican Post.

Five

Multi-Talented

Diane slowed to a stop at the restaurant. A tall, rotund guy with broad shoulders stood at the entrance gates. His smooth, dark hair was pulled back into a tail at the nape of his neck. He inserted a key into the lock on the glass door to the menu display on the tiled wall. Eric Jameson, Executive & Sous Chef was embroidered above the empty shirt pocket on his crisp, bright whites. His black thick-soled shoes boasted nary a drop of Alfredo sauce, which suggested he'd just come on duty.

"Hello, my dear," he greeted in a baritone voice. "Are you having a good day?"

"I am, thanks."

He gestured at the board. "This will be our menu for this evening. We open for fine dining at six p.m. Come join us." He drew on the slate board with colored chalk. Stylized leaves and a plump ripe tomato came first, then listed the selections as he spoke. "We'll warm up your palate with spinach salad, Mandarin oranges coated with mint dressing, and a cup of my tomato bisque soup."

He returned those chalks to the box and plucked the orange one to fashion a jolly, smiling shrimp. "Tonight's feature is fresh Mayport shrimp scampi doused with white wine kissed with garlic sauce, and grilled asparagus sprinkled with a flirty dash of datil pepper."

He repeated the chalk exchange and went on the next line where he drew a little snail wearing sunglasses. "Or, perhaps you'd like escargot nested in paprika seaweed and corn truffle seeded with black olive?"

Diane fell into a sort of temporary trance while her taste buds went nuts. "I'd like them all," floated out of her mouth.

"Good. We find our diners like to take their time over the rich Blue Mountain coffee I direct-buy from a farmer in Jamaica. It complements our Bananas Foster, or my key lime tartlet." He quickly pinched his fingers together, and extended his pinky finger. Touching his lips with them, he tossed an air kiss. "Apollo's personal sommelier, Ramon De La Corsica, offers the finest of wines, of course." The chef graced the menu with his signature. Finished, he returned the chalks to the box and snapped the lid shut. He shoved it into his pocket and pulled out a little gold key. He locked the glass door to the display and gave her his attention. Accolades were due.

"This is...amazing," she said with awe.

He chortled. "All in my day's work. May I ask, are you one of our guests?"

"Thank you for asking, Chef Jameson, but I'm not today. I'm here because...I've heard so much about Blue Wave I wanted to come see it for myself." Reciting half-truths when necessary was becoming easier for her in her work.

He lowered his voice with respect. "This resort's reputation is stellar. My kitchen is state-of-the-art. I make magic in it."

Not one shred of doubt crossed her mind. "Where did you study?"

"In Fort Lauderdale, Miami, and New York. Next stop for study is Rome, but I'm so busy I don't think it's going to happen." He winked. "Apollo keeps a close rein on us."

She smiled. "He knows quality when he sees it."

"And he can pay for it. His wife is also quite wealthy, and she likes this place. So to keep him happy she lets him have his head with it." He thought. "I must say he almost lives here."

"Well, thanks again. And I wonder if I may ask you a question or two?"

"Sure, and it's Chef Eric, please. I only have a few minutes—the vegetable truck arrived just as I came out here. I'll personally approve all foods before my staff puts them away."

"I'll try to keep it short." She brushed aside hair from her cheek. "I'm aware that Blue Wave recently lost a mermaid."

Chef Eric straightened and frowned. "Yes, yes, we did," he confirmed reverently. "Mermaid Nerissa was *more* than a *mermaid*. She'd become an institution. You didn't know her?"

She shook her head back and forth. "We moved into the area recently. I've taken on a new client who is related to her."

He raised his shaggy eyebrows. "A client?"

Diane opened her purse and gave him her card.

His eyes widened. "Ahh, now I understand."

Guests streamed past them, and one of them almost bumped into Chef Eric. He waved them off and waited for them to pass. "Do the police know you're following up on this?"

It was a pointed, but fair question, and he asked it politely. He'd also made good eye contact with her. She found him conversational, which made digging for facts easier and faster.

"I meet with Detective Brooks on a regular basis. Chelsea's grandmother is my client."

Chef Eric opened his arms. "Kitty Swan is one of our favorite diners. She comes in with one of her friends, usually June. I felt so sorry for her the night Mermaid Nerissa died." He checked his watch. "I felt sorry for all of us."

Diane stepped closer and softly asked point blank, "Do you have any idea who might've wanted to kill her?"

People's reactions to this blunt question yielded many stories. She watched carefully while Chef Eric's mouth tightened into a straight line and his eyes darkened. He searched her face. "Do you mind if we step away to discuss this?"

Diane held her ground. "Do you mind if we don't?"

Chef Eric sighed. "Yes. The walls have ears around here. Please?"

Sincerity and sadness filled his eyes.

"Okay, lead on."

He turned and steered her to the right. "Follow me to the ice room. We'll pass through the kitchen. If anybody asks, you want to order a sculpture and are interested in the process."

Diane shrugged lightly. "I didn't bring a jacket, and I *am* interested in the process. I've seen pictures of the King Neptune statue you made for last year's Summer Splash Bash. Your work is truly inspired."

Unabashed pride crossed his face. "It's a sideline. That design is now retired and won't be repeated, in memory of Mermaid Nerissa." They walked at a good clip, and Diane was at his mercy on knowing where things were located. She slipped in a quick text to Tom. *Am at Blue Wave, heading into an ice room with Chef Eric. XO.* No return text pinged as they passed more visitors and made two turns, which brought them into a rear corridor. It was well lit with rubber tile floors and bare walls. All the upscale fanciness was saved for the front of the house for show and guests.

Chef Eric slowed and jerked his thumb to the left. "In here." He pushed open the double stainless steel doors and ushered Diane into a large, noisy commercial kitchen. He quickly threw out a few comments to various underlings. Some of them sorted lettuce heads, or mashed mounds of red raspberries, while others cut carrots into star shapes. "I'll be in the ice room," he announced with authority. "Ralphita, handle whatever comes up until I come out. We'll be a short while. The lady here wants to better understand ice."

"Yes, Chef," Ralphita replied, whacking chicken breasts in half with a chunky knife.

Chef Eric yanked two reefer jackets and gloves off the hook by the door. Five freezing breaths later from inside the ice room, Diane donned one of the coats and zipped up the front. Obviously hardier than she, Eric left his to hang open. She put on the oversized gloves and looked down. The concrete floor had a blue tinge from a series of track lights overhead of the same shade alternating with clear LEDs.

Her breath puffed in front of her face as she walked toward large, translucent blocks of ice. Stacked together in a seamless fashion, the ice measured maybe six feet high and seven feet long and rested on wooden pallets. A work bench loaded with tools hugged the side wall on the right. Chain saws, a blow torch, and a steam iron rested on planks attached to the left side wall.

"Welcome to my other world," Chef Eric said, stepping over a hose that snaked over the floor around his feet.

Diane shivered. She'd definitely acclimated fast to the Florida climate. Anything below sixty degrees was bound to make her want a coat.

"Oh, it's nice. Um, how cold is it in here?"

"Climate controlled to twenty-eight degrees Fahrenheit."

"Let's keep this short, okay? Or my hands will fall off."

Chef Eric grinned. "You get used to it."

"Not me. Never." She pulled up the hood and her ears thanked her.

He walked over to the worktable and picked up two hand warmers and tossed them to her. She stuck them in the pockets and wrapped her gloved fingers around them. "Better, thanks. What're you working on here?" She nodded at the ice blocks.

"My next project. Come over and have a look." He turned on a light clipped to the side of the table and lifted a thin sheet of paper from the surface.

Passing a ladder leaning against the unsculpted ice, Diane arrived at his side. He taped the paper corners into place against the wood. She peered closer at the rendering on graph paper. "That's a lion. A very handsome one."

"Yes, ma'am. It'll be a gift from Apollo to the San Marco community for a special event honoring its history next week."

Her curiosity rose. "Why a lion?"

"They taunt power and symbolize St. Mark, who's the patron saint of Venice, Italy. That city inspired Mr. Stockton, the developer of San Marco, way back in the 1920s."

Diane marveled at the details on the paper. "You can get all that out of ice?"

His eyes lit up. "Each crease, fold, curve and line." He tapped the paper with his fingers. "What you see here is what the mayor will get."

Again, Diane was impressed with Chef Eric's talent. She and Tom had visited that community once since they arrived. Quaint shops, trees, crazy parking, and an old movie theatre had appealed to them both. A logistics question hit her. "How will you get it from here to there?"

"In pieces and in a refrigerated truck."

Diane continued her exploring. "What's that little chunk for?" She pointed to one that was about three feet by three feet on its own small pallet.

"It's a test block. I'm working with shimmers."

She looked at him quizzically.

"Those are additives to make ice shine, glow, and sparkle. Many are infused in the ice while it's being made and others are sprayed on. Colored neon lights can also be imbedded or added here. Or the sculpture can sit on a lighted base. Either way they add drama to the work and give it another dimension that changes while the piece melts. For example, the King Neptune statue you mentioned was fused from inside out with what I call 'diamond dust.'"

Kitty's photos sprang to Diane's mind. "No wonder it sparkles in pictures."

Chef Eric walked across to a workbench and tapped a large pickle jar full of what appeared to be glitter. "For Neptune, I'd used this finely ground mother of pearl extracted from the shells of mollusks like oysters and nautilus. The medium is iridescent and reflects light." He stepped over to the ice and gave it rap. "For the lion I'll create an internal luster with finely ground pyrite. He'll have a golden tone, and his mane and eyes will glisten."

Diane's sandaled feet reminded her why she shouldn't be in there very long. "I wish I could see more, but let's get back to Mermaid Nerissa. You have more to tell me?"

Chef Eric raised his hand in apology. "Chelsea was a complete darling for a long time. Then, she was getting a little unpredictable, one might say. Before she passed away, she seemed more serious and was withdrawing socially."

"Do you think she was afraid of something, someone?"

"It was more like she had the world on her shoulders. She wouldn't say why. It must've been personal, and I didn't pry."

"So, you were friends?"

"Work friends, yes. I often took lunch to her in the dressing room. She liked my version of peanut butter and jelly sandwiches on whole grain bread we bake here. They gave her an energy shot, and the way she worked, she needed them."

"I see. Is there anything else?"

He gave her an apprising look. "Out in the hall you'd asked me if I know who killed our star mermaid. Well, I wouldn't point fingers at anybody because I don't know who decided this planet would be better without her." He placed his fingers at his temple. "But...when something like this happens we wonder about things later."

"Often we do. Something that doesn't seem a bit out of the ordinary or surprising at the time can come back to us later and make us wonder. So, like what kind of things?"

Chef Eric stilled. "The night of her murder I took a shortcut through the passageway that runs behind the show tank. The dressing rooms are back there. When I passed by, she was yelling at someone. Nerissa was normally soft-spoken and didn't cuss. But this was full blast because something had riled her up good." He poked his finger against the corner of the ice. "But you know what? She was a total professional. She hit the water that night and positively rocked this place. You'd have never guessed she was under some kind of duress."

Diane momentarily forgot her chilled feet. "She mentioned no name in her rant?"

Chef Eric half shrugged. "I didn't hear one. I was on my way to the switchbox to turn on another set of lights for the ice sculpture. I do know she wasn't arguing with Hannah Hart or Owen Wagner. I ran into them together when I came out of the passageway at the other end."

He straightened a curl in the hose with his foot. "I might mention that it was no secret that Owen had a crush on Chelsea for a while. When she got engaged to that Luke guy, who's pretty damned full of himself, it sent Owen on multiple trips to a local beach bar when he was off-duty. One morning I picked him up from sleeping in the sand dunes all night. Better me to do it than the cops—or Apollo. Owen's ass would've been grass if he found him like that."

"How'd you hear about the engagement?"

"From Owen. Chelsea was hot, and he had eyes on her from the first day she started working."

"Did they ever go out together?"

"Twice, he'd said. He was making it into something he needed, I guess. Owen is gone now, but he had a steady girlfriend. So, all's well that ended well for him."

Pain prickled Diane's toes. She either stuck around and asked about some of the drills, prongs, picks, clamps, and chisels he used for sculpting, or she could kiss her two little toes good-bye. She pointed down at them. "I gotta go. My piggies are squealing." She winced over easing up on her professionalism.

Chef Eric gave a laugh. "Let's go the outdoor way."

"Thanks. I'll be back again soon. If anything else comes up, please let me know."

"My pleasure."

Six

Tom

In another twenty minutes, Diane drove her car and soaked up the delicious heat on A1A. Soon closer to home, she negotiated a left turn from Third Street and pulled into the Dairy Queen. Her craving for a hot fudge sundae had gotten the better of her.

Only thing, Tom wasn't with her. The hot fudge reminded her how she and Tom had met in the candy store in the Central West End at Christmas seven years ago. Now, after taking beach walks, they'd drop in here for a treat. Or else Tom took her to historic Pete's Bar for a beer.

Settled in the DQ table area, Diane checked her phone. Tom had messaged her. "Di, honey, don't panic, but yesterday I took a bullet. It passed right through my left palm. Lucky for me, eh? I'm coming home on medical for ten days. It's all I could get. See you tonight. I love you, T."

Suddenly, the hot fudge didn't taste so sweet. She lived with an ex-homicide detective who still courted danger every day in his new job at classified DeepSur2. Many women wouldn't invite that challenge into their life. But the saying, "Do the crime, do the time," ran thick through Tom's and her blood. Enough so that they stepped up to the plate and put elbow grease into making it a reality for thugs. Just how much elbow grease was up to each. Still, Tom getting shot curled Diane's toes.

~ * ~

Diane stayed up late in her dotted Swiss blue cotton robe and waited for her husband to come through the kitchen door. He'd called from the cab bringing him home from the airport. She had brewed fresh coffee and baked him a preacher cake, his new favorite. Kitty had given her the recipe and explained, "It's a Southern thing and was made for when the preacher came to visit."

Luckily, Diane found canned pineapple, pecans, and a bag of moist coconut in the pantry. Tom liked plain cake, so she blew off covering it with cream cheese frosting.

"Thank God it was his left hand," she said to herself.

To keep herself from conjuring up worse scenarios, she rehashed today's work. In retrospect, this had been a productive day for her. Yet, her visit to Blue Wave produced more questions than answers in the Mermaid Nerissa case. It would be this way for a while because she'd just begun trying to piece together the stubborn, unsolved case. *Unsolved* anything raised her hackles. Mounting details about the case niggled at her.

She pulled a small lamp from the sideboard to the kitchen table and draped the cord over the napkin holder. She switched on the lamp for better light and picked up Kitty's photo collection. One by one, Diane flipped through the nine pictures and paused over each one in her palm. She sensed one of them sported clues. If only she knew for what she was looking.

While she gazed at one of Kitty standing in front of Chef Eric's ice sculpture, the kitchen door burst open. She dropped the photos on the table and bolted from the chair.

"Tom!"

Her husband, wearing a sling, dragged himself into the room. His travel bag hit the floor with a thump. Wordless, he raised his bandaged hand, and opened his arms for her hug.

"Oh my goodness," she muffled into his neck. "Are you okay?"

He planted a kiss on her mouth, and she reveled in the moist warmth. She'd learned long ago not to make too big of a big fuss over him coming home scuffed up. Again, she tried to keep her emotions in check.

"God, I need you," he rasped. "My hand hurts like hell, but I already feel better."

"So do I."

Tom rarely showed vulnerability, but his voice was strained. His eyes shone with tired relief.

"Come sit," she added as she pulled out the second chair and he sank onto it. Leaning forward, he set his slinged arm and bandaged hand on the table for support. His well-planed face caught the lamplight as he spoke.

"The plane out of Tally was delayed, and…is that coffee I smell?"

Diane scooted to the cupboard for his favorite mug. "Coming right up with cake."

Tom nodded with a grateful smile. "You're the best. You really are."

Glancing at him over her shoulder, she busied herself at the counter. "You're not so bad yourself, luv." Her fingers shook a bit when she cut the cake, so the edges squiggled. She minded that more than Tom would.

"Thanks," he said when she set the coffee and dessert in front of him. "I…I need a pain pill. They're in my bag."

"Sure." She lugged the bag onto her empty chair. Unzipping it, she spotted black knit shirts he used for work and some underwear.

She also found a package wrapped in glossy white paper. By it lay a plastic bag with three amber plastic pill bottles, and she held it up questioningly.

"Yeah, those," Tom said, and motioned for her to open them for him. "I've been using my teeth to get the damned lids off."

Diane shook her head. "What'll we do about follow-up care?"

"The agency doc contacted a colleague at Mayo. I'll go over there to see him while I'm home."

She touched the bulbous white gauze bandage. "Is ten days enough?"

"Hardly, but it's the standard med time off. It can be extended if the doc requests it. Injury like this could be bandaged for five weeks." He turned his hand. "Thousand to one odds, but the slug zipped through fairly clean. No fractures."

She untwisted the lids and poured pills into her palm. "All these are for pain?"

"Nope. One's for pain. One's for infection. The other one is a pumped up vitamin. I'm low on magnesium and whatnot."

Diane handed the pills to Tom, and he swallowed them with coffee. Chasing smugglers had taken its toll. Stubble claimed his jaw, his shirt was wrinkled, and his jeans had a rip at the knee. Stylish for some, but it wasn't Tom's taste.

She returned the rumpled bag to the floor and sat next to him, not across like usual. Feeling his warmth made her realize how alone she'd been. She sipped some coffee and broke into her chunk of cake with a new fork and waved it at him. "Do you like?"

He clapped his good hand to his chest. "This is some kind of heaven you've got here."

She twisted the end of her hair. "It's close enough for government work," she joked and persisted with the wave. "How do you like the forks?"

He dropped his gaze to the one he held. "They look good. You've been shopping?"

"Kitty and I went to the Outlet Mall near St. Augustine not long after you left."

He grunted with satisfaction. "I brought you a present."

She raised the corners of her mouth. "I was hoping that was for me."

Tom gave her a mischievous nudge. "Who else would it be for? The dog we don't have?"

She laughed. "I've been meaning to talk to you about that. With you away more than ever now, I'm thinking of getting a cat."

Tom wrinkled his forehead in mock distress. "I'm being replaced by a feline?"

Diane raised her eyes ceilingward. "A female. Maybe a calico for company, comfort. I need something with me other than plants."

He turned his head toward her. "Let's think about it? I like dogs you know."

She bit into another forkful of cake. "I do know. But I'm away, too, and just like today there wasn't a chance to come home to let little Fido out."

Tom nodded. "Good point." He waved at the disheveled photo pile she'd left by the lamp. "What's all this? Someone's vacation pictures?"

Diane bit her lip. "They're from Kitty. She'd taken them the night of the murder at Blue Wave. I'm studying them for my new case. It's warming up, and I've got this deep, burning hunch there's a story somewhere in these."

He regarded her for a second, set down his mug, and picked up the one showing a guy in a tux in front of the King Neptune ice sculpture. "So what's cooking with this one?"

"He's Victor Chu, bartender at the swank Tiki Bar. I've not met him yet. See those purple dots on his white jacket lapel? Kitty says they're sequins from the costume Mermaid Nerissa wore in her last show before she died. Our question is how'd they get there?"

She picked up two more. "This one is of Apollo and Chelsea together earlier in the evening in front of the King Neptune sculpture. Chelsea was his cash cow and his favorite employee, so it's unlikely he pulled the plug on that. Then, this one's of Kitty also taken in front of the sculpture not long before she was supposed to meet Chelsea to go home. Kitty's still the walking wounded over this."

Tom nodded at the ice sculpture. "That's good work."

Diane agreed. "Yeah, and for carving up food and ice the way he does, Eric Jameson doesn't appear to have a mean bone in his body, and he respected Chelsea."

Perplexed all over again, Diane rested her chin on her hand and sighed. "In quick summary, this case is mushy. Detective Beau Brooks at the sheriff's office is making his best effort, but he's on overload. He and his team have missed something."

Tom reflected. "And you're going to find it. You're early in the game, and it's going to take some time. You know how some cases have a mind of their own. Then one day, bam! It's all there right in front of us. The body. The place. The time. The motive and the means. The perp comes to light with enough evidence to push it through the court without question. That's a big part of our jobs. Securing provable evidence for prosecution."

She moistened her lips. Even the thought of failure gave her the creeps. "In a perfect world, which is never mine. What I have is the body buried at Kirkland Cemetery. The place is the Blue Wave resort in Ponte Vedra Beach, which, by the way according to Kitty, used to be called Mineral City because minerals were mined from the sand and the area developed into a community after that."

"Wait," Tom interrupted. "About your trip to the ice room. I got your text, but couldn't reply. You were undoubtedly freezing in a back room with no windows, I assume, and alone with a stranger who could turn out to be Public Enemy Number One?"

She narrowed her eyes slightly at her husband. Was the gunshot he took making him super wary or over-protective? She prayed it wasn't so.

"It's off the kitchen and once was a storage room that Apollo had converted for Chef Eric for making ice and sculptures they use at special events. People saw us going in. There were panic bars inside on the two doors. I also still practice the new defense moves you taught me. My gut level told me it was okay to go with him because he was non-aggressive and said the 'walls have ears around here.' I was of sharp mind and have made a new contact. On my next visit, he'll most likely be happy to show me the Mermaid Dressing Room in the corridor that runs behind the performance tank. He'd heard the victim shouting at somebody the night she was murdered."

Tom locked his admiring gaze on her. "Never mind. Go on."

She swallowed. "The approximate time of death was ten-thirty. I have uncovered no real motive yet and identified no prime suspects to trail. Then, there's the sticky issue of an unidentified murder weapon and where it is."

Tom sat back in the chair. "That last item can screw it all up for you. Lack of evidence has gotten some bonafide trash off the hook."

Concerned, Diane folded her arms. "Yes, and you know how I don't like loose ends."

"Neither does a judge," he confirmed. "So you've got your work cut out for you. Meanwhile, why not open your present?"

Diane popped up from the chair and retrieved the gift from Tom's bag. Tugging open the ribbon, she tore away the paper. She flashed him a smile. "Chocolates."

The stressed glint in his cobalt eyes was fading. "Dark, just like you like."

Diane leaned over and kissed him on the cheek. "What would I do without you?"

Tom drew her to his chest and playfully whispered in her ear, "Snuggle a cat?"

Seven

True Love

The next day, Diane got up early and tended to Tom, making him breakfast and giving him pills, before she walked into her little office house. She brought along all her notes and Kitty's photos.

An hour later, she pinned the pictures onto the large cork crime board she'd hung up last week in what used to be a study with built-in shelves and a door that could be closed. Using an erasable felt-tip pen, she wrote questions and a To Do list on the white board next to it.

She was a visual person and kept things on which she worked in At-a-Glance sight. She'd devised color-coded string "connectors." She could attach one end of string to a note and the other end to pictures, clues, or "anomalies." The collection would grow.

These tools were admittedly homespun, but she liked the hands-on methods and had no trouble initiating computer searches to aid her investigations. Furthermore, Tom, Detective Brooks, and perhaps Kitty—with her fact-storing librarian mind and keen eye—stood by on tap.

She rechecked her interview plan and called Luke Talbot, Chelsea's boyfriend. After she introduced herself, she inquired if he had time to visit with her.

"Awesome," he said. "I have an opening from eleven until noon today. Will that work?"

She agreed, and he gave her directions to his dive shop in Jacksonville Beach. As it turned out, his place wasn't far from the public pier, and she made haste to his weathered wood door.

Stepping inside the little shake shingle-covered house on one of the turn-arounds, she found the place to be orderly. Colored air tanks stood on the floor in a corner and scuba diving magazines sat on the front counter where a cash register hung out with a laptop computer. Posters of divers underwater decorated the walls, and rock music played on the radio.

Luke walked into the room from a side doorway with *Employees Only* painted on the door.

"Hey, you're Ms. Phipps?"

Diane stepped forward and smiled. "I am, and you're Luke Talbot." The photo Kitty had shown her of him didn't do him justice.

"That'd be me," he said. "Good to meet you. We'll have fewer interruptions if we go back into my office. Out here, beach people walk in...and out...when they find out the bathroom is for customers only. Corky, my counter guy, can handle the front."

"If you wish. Quiet helps, and I'm glad we're getting to meet."

Corky sauntered into the room from a rear hallway. About thirty, he had shaggy ash blond hair, and wore shorts, flip-flops, and a florescent green Salt Life muscle shirt.

"Good morning, ma'am," he greeted and smiled. His teeth needed help.

She returned his kindness before she turned to Luke and followed him around the counter and down a short hall. At her first impression, Diane silently complimented Chelsea Graham for her good taste. Her fiancé's manner was polite, soulful, and signaled that he was a great listener. His handsome face and muscular frame undoubtedly turned heads.

As Diane settled in Luke's office, he shut the door. A pair of yellow flippers hung on the back and the rest of the room was a virtual closet stuffed with diving records and little black logbooks. A mariner's map of the coast of northeast Florida and southern Georgia hung the on the paneled wall. The owner-diver lifted his cell phone and turned off the ringer.

"First, would you like a cold soda?"

She declined the offer. "As you know, I'm here about Chelsea." Diane gave him a card.

He read it and dropped it on his desk.

Leveling his gaze on her, he said, "Good. Yes. *Somebody* needs to settle this case. The cops are doing their best, I guess. They hauled my ass in for questioning and figured out that was useless because I was off-shore that night with chartered divers." He lowered himself into his office chair and wheeled it closer to her. "In short, Ms Phipps, do I look like a friggin' murderer? No, certainly not. I didn't kill my girlfriend."

"Okay," she said calmly.

"And the twenty-thousand dollar reward her parents are offering isn't working. No tips and nothing conclusive have come out of it, as far as I know. This is a helluva situation." Before he sat down, he had raised his arms and let them free-fall to slap the khaki cargo shorts covering his thighs.

Diane changed her mind about the drink. "I'll take a diet, if you have it."

He slid his thumb over his eyebrow. "Sorry, there's no diet. I'm a hard-core purist when it comes to seafood, soda, and liquor. And I'll join you."

She nodded. Drinking alone never appealed to her anyway. He swiveled his chair and pulled two Cokes from the small refrigerator behind him. He popped open the ring tops and handed one can to her. "Bottoms up," he said.

Diane tilted her head back and let the cold liquid fizz over her tongue. Her gaze traveled up to the ceiling where a rattan fan swirled enough air to lift the corners of a yellow pad on Luke's desk. When it came to Luke, two questions blazed at about fifteen hundred watts in Diane's mind. Were he and Chelsea really engaged? Then, why have a secret engagement? But the man was sensitive and already fired up.

So she began with, "I'm hoping you'll clear up some of my confusion."

Luke folded his hands on the desk and looked her in the eye. "Bring it, because you're the second private investigator who's come to see me about Chelsea. I poured my guts out to that guy and never heard a thing since."

Diane's next breath collapsed. *Second private investigator?* She scrambled for poise.

"How long ago was this?" she asked without coughing.

"A month ago. I still have his card here somewhere." He opened the top right drawer of his desk and pulled it out. "Here you go. Louis Dresden, P.I., Flagler Beach, FL. His phone number is on here and e-mail."

Diane jotted the information down in her little notebook and handed the card back to Luke. *Focus on what's in front of you,* her inner voice demanded. "Well, I'll try to do it better. My client is Chelsea's grandmother. I'm wondering if you could tell me more about Chelsea around the time of the…tragedy."

Luke's voice softened. "My love was a mellow woman, happy, and balanced. In her work, she was driven, much like I am in my work. We got along well and made plans. But for some reason, she took a dive about a week before the Summer Splash Bash."

"A dive?"

He made a circular motion with his hand. "I mean, her mood hit bottom, and she wouldn't say what was wrong." Diane noted the frustration darkening his hazel eyes. It was time for her to dig deeper. How else could she put the whole picture together?

"The grapevine says you and Chelsea were secretly engaged. Was that true?"

Luke squeezed the soda can until it dented. "It was. We kept it a secret because we were going to elope a week after the Summer Splash Bash. Her father didn't like me, and her sister Gemma liked me even less."

Diane asked quietly, "Why all that, do you think?"

"Because her mom had a preppy son of a wealthy shipbuilder lined up for her. Chelsea couldn't stand him. Apparently, the guy shaved his legs." He snickered and took a breath. "Her sister was newly divorced and bitter. Owen Wagner overheard Chelsea and me talking late one night after her last show and let the cat out of the bag about us. Victor Chu and Owen were my fiancée's admirers. Men adored her."

Diane folded her hands in her lap. *Were they jealous enough to murder her...or him, for that matter?* "All that competition must've been a lot to handle."

Luke drank soda and wiped his mouth with the back of his hand. "It kept me on my toes, but it didn't bother me. She was a faithful girlfriend and not a trophy. And when you find out *who* did this insane thing, you better keep the creep away from me, or there'll be another murder!"

Diane half believed him. Cooped up passion tripped unbelievable switches. "I'll try to remember that. Until then, it seems Chelsea was popular at work and in her personal life. But do you know whom she might've had difficulties with?"

A double knock on the door stopped Luke in his tracks.

"Yeah, Corky. What's up?" he called.

Corky cracked open the door and gave it a slight push. "The city building inspectors are here. Routine, they say."

Luke rolled his eyes. "Okay, okay. Give me a minute." He squashed the soda can in his fist and tossed it into a tall trash bin.

Diane closed the cover to her little notebook. "It's all right, Mr. Talbot. I can come back."

Luke shook his head. "No, no. The answer to your question is that, aside from occasional flare-ups with Hannah Hart, her swimming double, or maybe the maintenance man for not replacing lightbulbs fast enough, Chelsea had no real nemesis or was involved in any feuds." He hesitated and added, "Except with her family...over me. Even that was cooling down. She was a grown woman and deserved to live her life the way she wanted."

Diane tended to agree. She was lucky her mother understood her drive to fight crime and shady dealings. But on her last birthday in January, she cheered a little louder, undoubtedly with relief her daughter had again made it to the party. She'd beat the high-risk odds for another year.

"More about Chelsea's moods," she said. "A delicate question, but I'm wondering if Chelsea was pregnant. It might have caused her to become overly sensitive or irritable."

Luke dropped an understanding gaze on her. "We weren't expecting, but we would've been happy about it. Kids were going to be part of our future together. But now..."

Diane couldn't avoid the sadness that swelled in her. One of the hallmarks of this job was how she encountered people struggling with life-long issues, regrets, and deep sadness. Luke was one of them.

"Of course, and I thank you." She rose from the chair. Turning toward the door, she dropped her soda can into the trash. Luke got up and closed the space between them as she returned to the hall. They re-entered the front area, and two official guys, each wearing a white shirt and black pants with a nameplate over his shirt pocket and an official-looking badge of sorts, waited for Luke. They brandished clipboards in their hands.

"Hey, Luke. This won't take long," the older one said.

"Thanks, Fred. I've got an appointment coming in at noon."

Diane scooted past them, and Luke opened the front door for her. She looked up at his frowning face. "I'm sorry this happened for you and Chelsea, and the truth will rise."

Luke's expression brightened. "I hope so. All I want now is for the piece of shit who murdered the love of my life to pay with their own."

"I'm on it," she assured him. Apparently, so was another P.I.! The prospect surprised her and nudged her competitive spirit.

Eight

How It Works

Several days later, Diane stood outside the dressing room Mermaid Nerissa had shared with Hannah Hart, now the headliner of Apollo's water show. The door was ajar and the lights on.

"Hello?" she called, but nobody answered.

Pushing the door open, she stepped inside the long, narrow room with a low ceiling.

A large mirror stretched over three kidney-shaped vanities. Each had its own chair. A photo of Hannah in her mermaid Salacia costume was clipped to the center mirror.

Directly above the cluster of make-up areas hung a long photo of Mermaid Nerissa reclining by the poolside. Wearing a tiara with starfish and shiny ribbons, she was in full costume with a miraculous pink, peach, and purple tail. Her blonde hair flowed over her shoulders and her purple bodice glittered in the light. A blue plaque beneath the photo was inscribed with *Forever In Memory.*

Diane lowered her gaze and glanced to her right to admire a plethora of costume bodices hanging on portable racks. To her left, colorful mermaid tails lay on the shelves of three metal carts supported with sturdy black wheels.

So this was Mermaid Nerissa's behind-the-scenes world. What troubles did it *really* hold? Diane pondered as she eased into the middle vanity chair. The door squeaked and Diane spun around to face it. Hannah Hart walked in and dropped her bag on a refreshment table.

"Hey, what're you doing in here and in my chair?" she asked ungently.

Diane pushed herself up and away. "Hello, I'm sorry to—"

"No, no, it's okay," she added. "But who are you?"

Diane gave her the usual introduction and handed the mermaid a card.

Hannah widened her eyes. "*You* are a private detective? I thought you were a fan. Sometimes I find them in here going through the drawers, if you can believe it. They've even taken things like our hairpieces, gum, bracelets, pens, and whatnot. I've complained to security, but they said to lock the door, and yadda, yadda, yadda." She gestured in the air. "So, I guess you're here about Mermaid Nerissa?"

Diane confirmed with a nod. "I wanted to meet you because you worked closely with Chelsea. I hope you'll have a little time to chat."

Hannah rested her hand on her hip and eyed her skeptically. Her auburn hair coasted down her back. Her blue shorts fit tight and her Jaguars T-shirt even tighter. She tossed her Boho bag on the chair Diane just vacated and placed her sunglasses on the vanity top.

"Okay. But I've met with the fuzz several times, once down at the station, and it all *still* is what it is. She was murdered and nobody knows why, right?"

Diane gave her a blunt, "Yes."

Hannah sighed and sank into her chair. "Have a seat, please. I don't like people standing over me," she said softly and indicated the one next to her. "I've got a rehearsal in twelve minutes, so we'll have to move this along, you know?"

Diane held her wince in check and took her up on the chair offer. Pulling out her little notebook, she said, "I'll make it quick."

Hannah gushed, "I just want you to know right up front, Chelsea and I were getting into it toward the end there. I mean, we got along well enough and all, but in her last days, she'd become very difficult to be around."

"What d'you think was wrong?"

"I don't know. She was about to run off to be married to Luke, and you'd think that would've made her happy. But not Mermaid Nerissa. Nope, she was getting testier and testier."

"Excuse me. You knew about their plans to elope?"

Hannah lowered her voice. "Yeah, but she didn't know I knew. I found out when I overheard her talking with Luke on their way out of here one night." She shook her head with confusion. "Chelsea had everything. You know what I mean? *Everything.* She got top pay here and extra gigs. She grew up in comfortable means and did what she loved."

Hannah counted on her fingers as she went on. "Apollo liked her...a lot. Victor Chu liked her. Owen Wagner once had a crush on her. Chef Eric liked her. Our wardrobe lady Rosa Delacroix liked her. She was a perfect size ten, by the way. Sam Lock groomed her into flawless performances. Even the maintenance guys liked her, and she gave them fits. Fans left her tips! So why was she so unhappy and...prickly?"

Diane wished she knew the answer. "Can you tell me about the last time you saw her?"

"Alive or dead? They wheeled her body out of here on a gurney."

Diane blinked. "Let's go with alive."

"Sure. We were in the tank for our last performance during the Summer Splash Bash. She almost missed two cues." She shrugged. "But it was at the end of the night and we were bone-tired. It takes a lot to lug around a heavy molded silicone tail, even in the water."

Diane made more notes. "I imagine so."

"As usual, we got a standing O," Hannah reflected.

"You can see that under the water?"

"Uh-huh. We have a circle of vision underwater. Anyway, Chelsea had a bad start that night, but pro that she was, she kept it under wraps pretty good. She had a killer smile."

Diane slid her gaze up to Mermaid Nerissa's face and dropped back to Hannah.

"Why a bad start that night?"

"She'd gotten a call from her sister, and it ended up in a yelling match. I'd seen that happen before, and you could've heard Chelsea out in the passageway."

Diane leaned forward. "So maybe family issues had been bothering her?"

Hannah checked herself in the mirror and began brushing her hair. "I suppose so. But she'd let things roll off real fast. Like the week before she died, we got into a tiff about our roles in the new productions coming up."

Diane knitted her eyebrows. "Hmm. That's a pretty big issue, isn't it?"

"It could've been worse," Hannah said. "She got the juicier roles because she was headliner. I kind of got tired of it and said something to Apollo. Then, Chelsea got upset over it, and…it wasn't right of me to go to him like I did."

She set down the brush and picked up a hot pink stress ball. She squeezed it in her hand. "I was hoping for a switch—just for one show a week—where I got trapped in the clamshell and was saved by Triton. But Apollo reminded me that I'm not as experienced as

Chelsea. She was two years older than me. She had put in hundreds of underwater hours more than me."

She changed hands for squeezing the ball. Her build and overall manner was more athletic than Chelsea's. "I lift weights. I can hold my breath under water for four and a half minutes. So I had quit dreaming about it, and Chelsea and I kept the blow-up between us." She ended with a slight smile. "The next week, we had a blast in St. Augustine for my birthday. And now…now I'm the headliner…and I miss her."

Diane dashed something else in her book and noticed a photo of a middle-aged couple on the vanity. "Are they your parents?"

"They are. I look a lot like my mom, everyone says."

"I'm sure they're proud of you…making it to top mermaid here at Blue Wave."

Her blue-green eyes took on a serious glint. "I'd do anything for them, to make them proud of me. Especially for my dad. I used to be shy, and he pushed me a lot to get better at things. He never handed out compliments much. Sometimes, my mom would tell him to lighten up. But it's changing, and I'm still not as good as Nerissa. But I'm much closer and almost at the top of the game in this industry."

Diane felt the pull of Hannah's charismatic energy. The girl had admirable passion and a goal. "You have everything going for you. I'll come see your show soon."

Hannah tossed aside the ball and thanked her. "When you do, come on back here after the performance, and I'll autograph your program for you." She beamed and half whispered. "I love saying that to people…that is, to the ones who don't break in here and go through my stuff."

Diane closed her notebook and stood. "That's understandable, and you can count on it."

The mermaid sped Diane a proud smile. "There are also postcards of me in the gift shop."

"I'll check them out."

Diane proffered her hand to Hannah for a shake and got a power squeeze in return. An alarm sounded off from the crystal clock on Hannah's vanity. "That's my reminder. I need to get suited up and report. Oh, and I've never met a lady private investigator before."

Amused, Diane replied, "I've never met a mermaid."

"We're a rare breed."

Diane could believe it. "Well, we come in all shapes, sizes, ages, and backgrounds."

"With all due respect, you can say *that* again."

"How so?"

"Because another PI—a guy—came through here about a month ago and asked me a bunch of annoying questions. Like, do I drink my coffee black. Do I have a dog, and do I take selfies five or more times every day and 'adjust' them before posting them online?"

Diane's middle tightened. She'd read recently that two of those might be indicators of disorders or psychopathology. Good old Facebook for quickie assumptions.

"Was he Louis Dresden?"

Hannah made a half turn on her way to plucking a black swimsuit off a hook. "Yeah, that was his name. He was gruff, smelled like tobacco, and dressed like a slob. I used magnolia air refresher in here after he left." A frown followed. "He asked me if I had killed Chelsea. Me? I don't kill sugar ants. What a jerk. Yes, Chelsea was getting to be a PIA, but there's therapy for that. Murder's kind of…outrageous, don't y'all think?"

Diane closed her notebook. "For most people it is, and it's highly illegal," she quipped. "I'll be off now. Can you tell me where I can find the Tiki Bar?"

Hannah supplied the directions. "There's a great view of the ocean up there. I go up after hours and sit. You can hear the breakers on the beach. Tell Victor I said hi."

Diane took one last look at the mirror and vanities. They all seemed so retro, and they did their jobs with a classy touch. Baskets of make-up and beauty products lay scattered about for quick service. Next to them lay a gold butterfly pin fastened to a cushion on the counter. She leaned toward it for a better view. "This is lovely," she murmured.

Hannah came to her side and picked it up. "I think so, too. It was Nerissa's. She wore it a lot. It's sort of funky, vintage. And now that she's gone, I'm giving it a home."

Diane moistened her lips. Torn, she touched one of the wings. "I know who gave this to her, and she has asked about it. So, now I can tell her it's in good hands."

"Her grandmother did. For good luck." She pulled the pin off the monogrammed towel and handed it to Diane. "When you see her Grandma Kitty next, just give it to her."

"Are you sure? It'd make her very happy."

Hannah rocked back on her bare heels. "Very. Nerissa's grandma probably needs this way more than I do. I've come a long way, Detective Phipps, in the last year and a half. I try to make my own luck, and I don't need a charm like this pin for good luck."

Nine

Good Samaritan

When Diane arrived at the Tiki Bar around 2:45, Victor Chu was opening the place for business. Patrons could either swim up for a drink or walk in for a tall seat at the counter until 2:00 a.m., if they wished.

"Hi, Victor," she said casually. She recognized him from Kitty's picture. His stout and medium stature, dark hair, skin, and eyes fit his Polynesian heritage, which she'd noted in Detective Brooks' reports.

"Hi, ma'am. We'll be open in fifteen, but you can have a seat now if you like."

Diane picked a tall stool on the corner. It gave her a better view of the ocean. Meanwhile, Victor jabbed orange slices with fancy toothpicks and dropped them back into a plastic bin.

"Are you enjoying your stay here?" he asked, obviously by rote.

Diane gave him the straight story. Victor frowned. "Not another visit from you guys."

"It's been busy?" Diane set her purse and cell phone on the bar top.

The bartender put on his jacket. "You could say that. It's been a swinging door here with detectives, another P.I., media people, and insurance investigators after we lost Nerissa last summer."

She raised her eyebrows. "For good reason."

"I wouldn't argue that." He pointed at his mouth. "But please read my lips. I don't know who killed Mermaid Nerissa. I only know that I *didn't* do it, although it crossed my mind a few times." He paused. "Only figuratively, that is."

Diane crossed her arms. "Okay."

He pushed his fingers through his black hair and gave her a look. "You're easy to please."

He was thirty-five and trim-waisted. His tropical shirt collar lay open at the neck, and his name badge was about to slide off his ecru lightweight jacket with the sleeves rolled up.

"Maybe. You're losing something," she offered and pointed at it.

Victor glanced down and made the save. "So, here's the thing. The night Mermaid Nerissa died, she wanted extra help with her costume after the show. She said she couldn't depend on Hannah to help her, so I did her the favor."

Diane made a mental note. "That was nice of you."

The bartender barely smiled. "She had exited the performance tank on the travel tube end of the tank after her final call."

"Wait. There's more than one way to get into the water?"

Victor held up two fingers. "Pay attention, please. There are two. Swimmers can drop in from the ledge along the top of the back of the tank in Neptune's Grotto. Or, depending on the choreography, they can get in or out at the small tank that's hidden behind the stone wall nearest the ice sculpture.

The plexiglass tube that runs through the ceiling connects the two tanks. It's a great effect. At either end, the mermaids can pull themselves up out of the water and sit on a platform to take off their tail. Then they drop it over the edge behind them, and it lands on a foam mattress to be picked up. There's a ladder on the outside of each tank for the performers to climb safely down to the floor. It's about an eight foot drop."

"I see. Who knew?" Apollo's attention to detail really did impress her.

Victor ran a white towel down the bar top. "They're out of sight on purpose, but people who work here know."

"It seems a maze here. One can get lost pretty quick. Go on, please."

"There's an alcove near the ice sculpture, and I was clearing empty glasses from some of Apollo's private party friends. When I passed by the entrance to the tube exit platform room, Mermaid Nerissa caught me and asked if I would carry her top and tail back to her dressing room. By then, she'd changed into her red bathing suit." He stalled for a minute. "Damn, that girl was sweet and could fill out a suit. I just wished..." his voice trailed off.

Diane lifted her fingers to her chin. "You wished for what?"

Victor cocked his head to one side, snapped the towel, and dropped it into what looked like a trash bin. "It's personal, Ms. Phipps."

Diane snared his gaze. "There, there. Everything's personal when it comes to murder."

"Thanks for that," he retorted. "But for the record, I secretly wished she was my girl. I never made a move on her, though. Love at work screws with your day...and could with your pay."

Diane admired his honesty. "Even though she was 'difficult' toward the end?"

He laughed. "Hell, she just needed a good man is all. We'd have worked it out if it ever really amounted to anything."

"Didn't she have a good man? Luke Talbot."

Victor pushed a bin of glasses in her direction. "That'd be 'yes.' Her best friend had given her a gift certificate for scuba lessons. Then

I had to find me another dream lover." He whipped a clean cloth off a stack and wrapped it around his hand. "Want to help me polish?"

Unruffled, Diane declined. "I'll pass. I'm here only for a few minutes, remember?"

Victor snickered. "I was joking."

Diane didn't think so. "So why couldn't Chelsea depend on Hannah to bring her stuff back to the dressing room for her? Was that a big deal?"

"I don't know why, except that night was crazy. So many people everywhere." He turned on a blue neon sign for Blue Moon beer. "Maybe it was just an off night for them where they weren't seeing eye-to-eye. The wardrobe mistress, Rosa Delacroix, usually picked up the mermaid tails and carted them over to the dressing room for storing. But that night Rosa was busy giving out free leis to guests. So Mermaid Nerissa asked for my help."

"I saw the tails today. They're amazing."

"And they're expensive, custom-made originals to fit each mermaid perfectly. Heaven help the mermaids if they gain five pounds. Back to the point, their swim tails can't be left about…*anywhere*. They can sprout legs faster than tadpoles, if you get my gist."

It was getting warmer outside, and Diane's mouth was going dry. "I certainly do."

"Especially in your line of work." He chuckled.

"May I have a bottled water, please?"

Victor checked his watch. "The register wakes up in four minutes. But since you're a minion of the law, I'll put it on my tab."

"Kind of you, but I don't accept gifts on the job."

The bartender walked down about three feet, slid open the lid to a steel case, and brought the water back to her. "Have it your way. You can pay me in three minutes and fifteen seconds."

She untwisted the lid and drank. "Now, just for the record, the last time you saw Mermaid Nerissa alive was in the small tank room?"

Victor leaned over and turned on a radio on the bar. "Nope. The last time I saw her was a half hour later. She was heading into Neptune's Grotto. The door stuck, and I helped her with it. After that, I went back out to the pool area. Apollo was giving away comp tickets to our shows, and he'd ask me to help give them to the winners. They love that."

Diane's curiosity piqued. "Why was Chelsea going into Neptune's Grotto? Wasn't it closed for the night?"

Victor gave her a full nod. "I guess she forgot something in there, or maybe she wanted to meet someone. And that's all I know. I swear." His eyes never drifted from hers. He blinked normally, and his body language didn't reveal a phony move. No warning dings went off for her intuition. She'd bet her Class G Florida firearms license the guy was on the level. Time had come for her to move on. But her prospect list was getting shorter.

Diane collected her purse and cell phone. "I need to go." She opened the purse and pulled out some cash and left it on the bar. "Thanks, Victor Chu. And Hannah says hi." For a brief moment, she watched the sea. *Mermaid Nerissa was going to meet someone, all right. Her killer.*

Ten

Dead End

On her way out of Blue Wave, Diane stopped at the gift shop. Lit marquis from the water shows studded the walls. She gazed at each showing the swimming cast appearing in their places for final bows and lights out at the end of the show.

She purchased one showing the whole cast and one of Hannah's postcards. She was known as Mermaid Salacia, so named after Neptune's queen. Diane paid for the cards, tucked them into her notebook, and drove north back up A1A.

Late afternoon light played through the live oaks and palms and shed a golden glow on whatever it touched, making one section of the road seem surreal. Facts from a booklet Kitty had put in a welcome basket for Diane and Tom came back to Diane.

Hard to imagine, but fourteen thousand years ago, Florida was double its size and dry prairie. Pre-historic People of the Shell Mounds lived among mastodons, horses, bison, wooly mammoth, and camels that freely roamed in this area. Rising waters eventually had crept inward and covered much of the beaches and many pre-historic sites.

Diane stopped for a few errands and made it home to find Tom in the kitchen making spaghetti. "Are we out of oregano?" he asked after he gave her a peck on the cheek.

"We're not." She pointed to one of the grocery sacks. "You must be feeling better."

He threw her a sexy wink. "Hey, you can't keep a good man down, Mrs. Phipps."

Her heart filled with warmth. The pain in his hand was under control, and he was sleeping better. It did her good to see Tom relaxed, wearing beach shorts and a t-shirt. It did her good to know he'd be home tonight, too. The pulse of her life changed when he was around.

By nine o'clock they sat out on the patio, each having red wine.

Tom wrapped his fingers around hers. "What's up?"

Diane sighed. "What do you mean?" she replied softly, thinking of her case.

"You're worried about something."

Diane nodded slightly. "You were right. This one's going to take time to unravel."

Tom let go of her hand and half-turned toward her. "When would that stop you?"

She set down her wine glass and pushed herself up from the lounge chair. "Probably, never." She stepped over to a potted hibiscus, pinched off a dying bloom, and dropped it onto the mulch.

"There's something else," she added. "I've got some competition. From what I'm hearing, he sounds like a dime-store gumshoe. When I check in with Detective Brooks next, I'll bring it up. Somebody hired the guy. Other than that, I found out how the sequins got on Victor Chu's coat. Chelsea had some serious secret admirers, and I now have Chelsea's butterfly pin that Kitty had given her."

"How'd that happen?"

Diane sat down next to him again. "Hannah Hart had it and asked me to give it to Kitty." Her thoughts strayed back to Hannah. "She's Number One now and is handling the notoriety well, I think." She picked up her wine glass again and ran her finger around the rim. "I also learned that something was up with Chelsea. Almost everyone noticed a change in her not long before she died. Whatever was bothering her had robbed her of her good humor."

Tom crooked an eyebrow. "Sounds serious. Maybe she told Kitty?"

Diane rested her head against the back of the chair. "Chelsea kept it totally mum."

Diane's cell phone rang and she scooped it up from the arm of the chair.

"Hello, Kitty. Yes, Tom's better, and I have something for you. Sure, I can have coffee in the morning. See you then. Okay, I'll tell him. Sleep tight."

She hung up as Tom finished off his glass of wine. "Kitty sends her regards."

Tom gave her a nod. "I ran into her at lunch at the golf club today. She was coming in with a group of women wearing red hats. She stopped by my table and made some fuss." He lifted his hand, which still sported a bandage wrap.

Diane explained the hats, and, "She's a good person."

Tom went on. "There's more there than meets the eye."

"How so?"

"She was carrying a little photo album for their Throwback lunch. There was a photo of her on the cover. Did you know that our friend Kitty was in a rock band?"

Diane threw her head back and laughed. "People never cease to surprise me. You think you know a person, then boom…you find out there's this whole other side to them that somehow doesn't match up right."

Tom shrugged. "People go through stages. They're at one place one day in their heads and hearts, but not the next. Take me, for example. I used to want to be a tightrope walker."

Diane swung her head in his direction. "When you were ten?"

"Twelve. I practiced out in our back yard and could go twenty feet without falling off the cable. That was before I wanted to be a fireman. Later, when the honor scholarship came through for college, criminal justice became my forever home." A rueful glint sparkled in his eyes. "That's my story, sweetheart, what's yours?"

Diane pulled her knees up close to her chin and wrapped her arms around her legs. "For a while, I lost all modesty and was a model for an art class."

Tom whistled and teased, "Wow. Do you have throwback pictures of that?"

She giggled. "Hush. It kept me in Ramen and college clothes during my sophomore year."

"Actually, people do the darndest, most unlikely things for money."

"They sure do," she put in. "Like kill people."

That brash thought crashed into her head like a big cold ocean wave. She flattened her legs and sat up straight. "I need to go see Kitty."

"Now? It's almost ten o'clock."

She pushed herself to her feet. "Yeah, she stays up late to do jigsaw puzzles. But I'll call her first. You don't mind, right?"

Tom heaved an exaggerated sigh. "A detective's work is never done—go."

She leaned over and kissed him. "Go rest, okay?"

"I'll wait up."

~ * ~

Twelve minutes later, Diane rang the bell on Kitty's front door, and she opened it with a flourish. It was no secret Kitty adored having company. Diane returned her smile and brief hug.

Kitty chirped, "Hi, come on in. I've been working on a new Ravensberger puzzle. It has fifteen hundred pieces and is a doozie. So, let's go to the den where we can talk." She steered Diane in that direction, and added, "I hope you have new things to share with me."

Diane couldn't overlook the yearning in Kitty's eyes. "I've learned a few things and have some new information bearing on the case."

Kitty's eyes flickered. "But no suspect?"

"Not yet…but I'll keep at it. I don't drop cases."

"Thank you," Kitty said softly.

Diane left it at that for the moment, silently debating what to share and what not. She followed her hostess into the den. Kitty looked comfortable in her pink cotton pajamas with creases in the pants. A floral embroidered motif accented the edges of the two small flat pockets on the top. Creamy smooth satin slippers covered her feet, and her hair was tied back and held in place with a narrow black ribbon.

Diane was beginning to think Kitty looked superb at any time and in the face of adversity. She secretly wished for such panache. Her hair was mussed, lipstick worn off, and a shower awaited her. But Kitty gave her no ill looks.

"Here, pull up a chair," Kitty said, approaching the table she'd set up for the puzzle. "I'm putting together the outside edges now. You can help me sort pieces, if you like."

Diane settled on Kitty's right and widened her eyes at the puzzle. "I've never done this."

Kitty showed her what to look for. "They'll have straight edges like these." She lifted a sample as Diane looked at the box showing the colorful picture.

"Gosh, this is intricate."

"It's called Atrium Garden and will be my third. I started doing them not long after my husband, John, died three years ago. They keep me and my mind busy. I'll watch TV while I do them sometimes."

"What do you do with them after they're finished?"

"I seal them and frame them and give them as gifts. Iced tea? It's caffeine-free green tea. Won't keep you awake." Kitty pulled a pitcher of it closer to her.

Diane nodded. "Lovely, thanks."

While Kitty poured, Diane said, "Before we get started, I have something for you." She slipped her hand into her shorts pocket and pulled out the item wrapped in lime green tissue. "I think it'll make you happy, Kitty. And there are some other things, too."

Kitty settled her gentle gaze on Diane. "I can't thank you enough for taking on this case. While I'm working in the garden, I see you driving by. I pray that this will be the day that you'll come back with irrefutable truth and answers, so justice can be done. Chelsea didn't deserve to die."

Diane handed her the pat of tissue and Kitty opened it slowly.

Kitty's face went from a frown to a brilliant, grateful smile. She cradled the pin in her palm, which began to shake. "Oh, my gosh….it's my butterfly pin, the one I gave to Chelsea."

Pleased, Diane sat back in the folding chair. "It belongs here with you."

Kitty pinned the butterfly on her pajama top. Her composure soon returned with the help of Kleenex and kind words from Diane. "Also, the sequins from Chelsea's costume were on Victor Chu's jacket because he had carried it back to the dressing room for her."

Her friend listened quietly. "I see. It did bother me."

Diane hesitated, then said, "There's more. You were right. Luke did want to marry Chelsea." She took a breath. "They were engaged. Chelsea was heading into a happy future."

Kitty's jaw dropped. "Engaged? Praise be." Her eyes watered up again.

"I still don't know what was bothering her so much, and I may never find out." She took in some tea. "It is sort of late, but I have another question to ask about Chelsea."

Kitty gushed around a new tissue, "I'll not sleep if we put it off. Please, go ahead. What's on your mind?"

Diane began sorting puzzle pieces. "I'm wondering if Chelsea had a life insurance policy."

Kitty tucked the tissue up her sleeve and pushed puzzle pieces this way and that. "Oh, my dear, yes. She was well-insured. Apollo also required her to have a policy when she began working at Blue Wave. Undoubtedly, he had special insurance on her and the rest of the cast because of the nature of the shows."

Diane pursued this line of questioning. "Do you happen to know who her beneficiaries were?"

Kitty raised her fingers over the puzzle pieces. "Her family, me, and her best friend Jennifer." She lifted one and fit it into the growing frame that was well on its way to making a large rectangle. "There was a lot of money, Diane. She loved every one of us. If she and Luke had made it down the aisle, her policy would've changed. But at that time, she had named those of us closest to her." Kitty looked away for a few seconds. "I'm donating most of my portion to UNF for scholarships in her name."

Diane swallowed. She saw so many disregards for people's lives in her work, but Kitty's kindness bolstered her faith in humankind. "Just to make sure, there was no will?"

"There was none that I know of." She pointed to the puzzle picture. "If you find any green ones like that, they go at the bottom of the frame on your side of the table. And if you see any orange ones, they'll go over here on mine."

Kitty's resilience amazed Diane. If she were in Kitty's shoes, having lost Tom and a granddaughter, she'd probably fall into a deep hole and wither away.

Kitty must have caught her admiring gaze. "For a quite a while, I went for grief counseling. I need it much less now. Although I want the killer found, prosecuted, and sentenced, I'm learning to accept all this because I *have* to. There's still a lot of beauty in this world."

Diane squeezed her hand. "You're an inspiration."

Kitty smiled. "I'm motivated, because I really want to be around to sign a check to you."

Another forty-five minutes passed, and by the time she left, they had completed constructing the outside edges of the puzzle. Walking home, Diane realized how much jigsaw puzzles were similar to solving cases. Facts fit together to form the whole big picture. She opened the front door and walked through the foyer to the living room. Tom looked up from reading in his favorite chair.

"How'd it go, Ms. Sherlock?"

Unsmiling, Diane sank down on the hassock by his feet. "Kitty's quite the lady, and it looks like insurance money wasn't the motive."

"There were no greedy beneficiaries who hated her enough?"

Diane shook her head from side to side. "Her best friend was true blue, according to Detective Brooks. She'd disappointed her family by falling in love with Luke, but no one was upset enough to do her in. Solid alibis, all of them."

"They could've found someone to help them out with that." He gestured a pointing gun and added, "Pop."

She smiled somewhat. "So, it seems I've reached another dead end with the insurance money angle." She soon sighed. "I have a lot to go yet, don't I?"

Tom leaned over and laid his hands gently on her shoulders. "Tomorrow's a new day, P.I."

Eleven

Another P.I. and Clues!

Diane walked into the S.O. and found Detective Beau Brooks sitting at his cluttered desk. He ate chow mein with chopsticks from a white box. "Good to see you," he said. "How's it going on the mermaid case?"

"Thanks. I'm still fact finding and meeting people who were in her life." She sat in the chair next to his desk. "Say, could I spend a little more time with the case files? I might have some new notes to add."

Brooks dropped the chopsticks into the empty box and set it aside. He looked like he'd been up all night. "We'd love new notes—when we can get them." He scribbled a pass for her for the records clerk and handed it to her. Her name was spelled wrong, but she wasn't going to quibble.

His phone rang, and he raised a finger for her to wait.

The noise in the room buzzed around her. It used to be this way in the department where she'd once worked on fraud cases in St. Louis. Not enough room to spread out, and stale air circulated. But those days were gone for her, thank heavens. She enjoyed the fairly newfound autonomy in her work life too much to grin and bear regular job structure anymore.

Crossing her legs, she adjusted the hem of her short, casual skirt. She moved the ringer button to Off on her cell phone and let her gaze wander. But not too far. At about forty, Detective Brooks was a fine-looking guy. His dark hair almost touched his shirt collar, and his deep blue eyes gave a hint of wisdom from having seen it all. He had a strong jaw with a dash of stubble, too, and a straight mouth. His short-sleeved tan knit shirt hugged his broad shoulders and exposed a good part of his biceps. A department-issued badge was clipped to the belt that encircled his waist, and his black pants fit him to a T. His name and the official logo of the St. John's County Sheriff's Office were embroidered on the shirt. There was no question in Diane's mind that he worked out...a lot.

Two tickets to a Jacksonville Jumbo Shrimp baseball game lay on a pile of reports, records, and forms by the computer screen. Most of the buttons blinked on his multi-line phone. Above it hung a photograph of an attractive woman and a curly-haired child on the beach. It had been ripped in half at one time and taped back together. That was it for the personal side of Detective Beau Brooks.

He banged down the phone receiver. "Damn, they've *misplaced* an evidence bag," he growled and looked at her with ire in his eyes. "No case will stick in Judge Watson's court without properly documented and relevant evidence." He closed his eyes briefly, raised his palms toward her, and reopened his eyes. "Sorry."

Diane smiled. "I understand, and I'm—"

"Still working on case number seven-six-three-one-five."

"That's the one, yes," she answered bluntly and pulled out her little notebook. "I have a question for you."

"Shoot." He gave her a wry grin.

"Two people I interviewed, Luke Talbot and Hannah Hart, mentioned that another private detective had visited them about

Mermaid Nerissa. So, I...I wanted to know if you have a duo working out there on this, and if we'll get together for a meeting? You know, to fill you in and compare notes?" She kept her tone professional, but her ego was quietly taking a hit.

A full belly laugh erupted from Detective Brooks. On one hand it was actually good to see the strain on his face disappear. On the other, he shocked her.

"Let me guess," he finally said. "His name is Louis Dresden."

Diane moistened her dry lips. "That's him."

He raised an eyebrow. "How long ago was it that he'd paid visits?"

"Probably a month and a half," she answered, frowning. "They described some of his raunchy methods. It all threw me a little, Detective."

"It should've. He's a con artist. We've been trying to catch him in the act."

Stunned, Diane repeated, "Con artist?"

Detective Brooks rolled his chair back and stood. He was every bit of six foot two and towered over her. "His real name is Bight Kepler. He shows up during homicide investigations and tags people who were connected to the victims, gets information, and leaves."

"You mean like I do?" regrettably slipped from her tongue.

Brooks laid a parental gaze on her. "Now, now, Ms. Phipps. You're doing it legally. And you're not leaving...are you?"

Diane confirmed. "Not any time soon."

"He's a phantom. He changes his appearance, strikes and is gone."

"His card shows he's from Flagler Beach."

"Yeah, and my Aunt Flossie is a nineteen year-old White House aide."

Diane smirked and straightened her shoulders. "Why doesn't he share what he finds out with you to help convict Chelsea's murderer? That way he can collect the twenty-thousand dollar reward."

Suddenly, she felt naïve in the quiet beat that followed. What criminal mind would work like that? It was too…honest. At least, Brooks saved her from reminding her of it out loud.

"So what's he doing with the information?" she pressed.

The detective hung his hand at his waist. "At first, we thought he was selling it…to people like me and you, insurance companies, or relatives who were desperate or pressured enough to buy into that bull. But my contact in Miami reported that he's out for collecting general dirt. When or if it's dicey enough, he blackmails those involved."

Diane shook her head. "Hmm. A blackmailing, criminal impersonator. Active in this area." More trouble in paradise, she thought with regret.

"There's a lot of homicide in this country, and people like to keep their misdeeds under wraps," Brooks remarked. "Kepler gets around."

"How'd your contact find out about the blackmail?"

The detective sighed heavily. "His daughter Francie was a friend of a med-school homicide victim. Francie had cheated on a test in med school and didn't want it to get out and about. After making two payments in cash to Kepler through a P.O. box, she owned up to it with her dad. Kepler didn't know he was an FBI agent, and a stakeout for the box was set. But Kepler never showed up for another pickup. The dude had skipped."

Diane's heart thumped. She hated hearing about values going awry within law enforcement families. "What happened to Francie?"

Detective Brooks moved to his desk and picked up his coffee mug with Beau printed on it in big red letters. "She got a reprimand from her family and a temporary suspension from school. She now keeps clean and works in an E.R. in Philadelphia."

He lifted the mug and threw down some coffee. "Crap. This is cold." He set it down with a thud and nodded at her. "If you run into our friend Dresden, contact me right away. Meanwhile, carry on, Ms. Phipps. The records clerk will give you the password for the computer down there. An anonymous tip came through last week that I added to the online file."

Diane rose from the chair. "A tip?"

"A dead one—like all the rest of them, but until this case is closed, nothing is really dead."

She slung her purse strap over her shoulder. "Except for the victim."

Detective Brooks wagged a finger at her. "You have dry wit, but I like it." His expression hardened. "Stay vigilant. You're pushing somebody's buttons, believe me."

Diane flashed him her cell phone. "You're on my speed dial, and whose button do you think I'm pushing?"

The detective lowered his voice. "Eric Jameson, the ice man who can cook a perfect steak. Something about him doesn't ring true, but his alibi is solid."

She looked at him quizzically. "Why him?"

"Because according to some new intel that came through yesterday, he owed Mermaid Nerissa a chunk of cash and never mentioned it to me or my team."

"Nor me."

"Maybe she got tired waiting for it and it made him nervous?" His suggestion hung in mid-air. His phone rang again and he snatched up the receiver. "Detective Brooks. Okay, I'm on it." He dropped the receiver and plucked his holster and Glock .40 caliber from the coat rack. "Happy hunting, and keep me informed."

~ * ~

Diane adjusted the goose neck lamp on the table downstairs in Records and opened bank storage box number seven, which was full of the Mermaid Nerissa case records. She sorted through incident follow-ups, first responder reports, news clippings, the medical report, ID notes, briefing notes, and crime scene photos.

The medical examiner's report had been recently amended, and she pulled it out first to recheck his findings. A physical description of Chelsea lay before her eyes, along with *Apparent Cause of Death: Stab wound to right carotid artery. Lacerations on victim's neck. Flesh was torn at right angles, suggesting that the wound was caused by a round dowel or smooth prong with possible barbs at the end. Suspect is right-handed. Victim bled to death. No tissue under nails. No bruises, except at point of entry; no struggle occurred. Murder weapon inconclusively identified and unfound."*

The photos in Diane's hand nearly turned her stomach. Chelsea didn't have a chance to survive that kind of attack. She studied the collection of crime scene photos again, including one that showed the bloody streak blazing diagonally across the aqua tank glass.

ID department had listed only one set of fingerprints on the whole of the glass. They belonged to Chelsea. Apparently, she'd laid her hand against the glass…gently, as it was a light print. In comparison, the single finger print was heavy and broad, making her print size larger.

The round part was at the top. As her finger trailed down the glass it became faint, as if her finger had dropped away at the end. Diane shuddered. It had to be her moment of death.

Next, she opened the new addendum to the original report. She read aloud, "Traces of calcium carbonate crystalline aragonite present in the wound. Confirmed by Holcomb Forensic Labs, Roanoke, VA, May 5, this year."

Diane had no idea what that was and entered it into her little notebook. Perhaps Tom would know. He still kept abreast on substances, poisons, acids, and other hazardous chemicals and metal filings. More than once, his knowledge of them had sealed cases tighter than a tomb.

Her next question was why did the addendum turn up now? She got up from the chair and asked the records clerk, who wore large glasses and a scaled down uniform. Charlotte was printed on her nametag with a felt tip marker. She checked the date of the original report and the date stamp from the recent update from the lab. Her accent was deeply southern.

"I reckon this addendum was misdirected to a police station in Cincinnati, and they sent it back to the lab. For some reason, they sat on it until Mildred Farmington; our county medical examiner, followed up on it and put in a new request. How's that for up north service, Missy?"

Painfully slow, Diane scorned to herself and supplied a quick smile.

"Thanks."

The important thing was she was looking at a confirmed clue. She could trace the source of the substance once she learned what the stuff was. She returned to the table and reread the pages in one of the fat reports held together at the top with shiny Acco Fasteners.

In some ways, current crime investigation had evolved into new dimensions and techniques. In others, they stood still. She also accessed the online files regarding the case. Re-reading them produced no new results. Detective Brooks and his team had worked thoroughly. Every tip was checked out. Every alibi stuck. How maddening!

Twelve

Perfection

The next day, another trip to Blue Wave put Diane in touch with Sam Lock, the show choreographer. They met poolside, and she made her usual introduction. He soon shared that Apollo had hand-picked him from a plethora of applicants who had applied for the job at the opening of Neptune's Grotto.

He'd arrived on the scene with strong credentials, including Las Vegas productions. His tropical shirt, featuring hula girls, hung loose and dropped to mid-thigh, half covering blazing blue shorts. A Kuki nut ring hung around his neck. His sandy-colored hair thinned in front.

She couldn't see his eyes behind his reflective pilot sunglasses. That hampered her ability to catch glimpses of him through the window to his soul. But she forged ahead.

"I've heard you were making the rounds," he said, tenting his fingertips together. "I guess my number's come up?" The classic steepled position of his hands often translated into authority and power. No show existed without a choreographer who called all the shots. Yet his friendly tone of voice put her at ease.

She gazed at him from beneath the brim of her beach hat. "Maybe it has," she said. "I'm here officially to talk with you about Mermaid Nerissa, if you don't mind?"

Sam separated his hands and opened his arms. "Of course, and I officially don't mind, Ms. Phipps."

"Good." She liked to get that point out of the way early in her interviews. The fact remained that not one person *had* to agree to talk with her. No SJSO citations would be issued for not helping her. Florida lightning wouldn't strike, either. But she was an avid notetaker and respectful of time. She kept her questions on point, and someone's conscience might come up for air when all was settled.

"How was working with Mermaid Nerissa?" she asked and smiled.

Sam leaned back with a typical man-spread and clasped his hands behind his neck. "Enjoyable, usually. The lady had class. She had good timing, performance presence, and could make difficult moves look easy. She had a sense of humor, too, and playfulness about her. Her positive attitude helped her be a winner. I only had to prod her occasionally about form, but it wasn't a problem. She never missed a performance without notice. Except for a little glitch, her last one exceeded all my expectations. Other than that, it was if the hand of God was leading her through it."

"How so?"

Sam shrugged. "She becomes one with the water. The glitch during her last show was just a hiccup, really. Unnoticeable to the untrained eye. Things can get out of sync fast and mess with a whole scenario we'd worked on for weeks. It happened during her final flip and triple twist. Delayed, it threw off the next cue a shade."

Diane wrote quickly. "Where do you think she would've been five years from now?"

"That's no mystery. She'd be married to Luke What's-His-Name, for one thing. She'd be the mother of his children and maybe juggling her career at the same time if she decided to stick with it. More and more private requests were coming in the door."

"Impressive."

"Truthfully, in five years she wouldn't have needed me or this gig at Blue Wave."

Diane raised her eyes to him. "You were a part of her phenomenal success."

Sam lowered his arms. "True to a point. But she walked in the door with plenty of drive and was getting creative about her moves. We collaborated on story content and music. Searching for Neptune's Secret was initially her idea." He snapped his thumb and fingers, hailing a bronze-skinned server wearing a two-piece bathing suit. "How about you bring us two scotches on the rocks?"

"Happy to, Sam."

Diane raised her hand. "Thank you, and none for me."

Sam lowered his sunglasses. His dark brown eyes twinkled. "Honey, this is beach country. We drink and work, eat seafood, stroll the beach, shag each other if we want, and protect sea turtles, all in mixed fashion."

Sleuth Diane drew in a jostled breath. "Looks like I've a lot to learn."

Sam grinned. "We won't hold that against you, princess. Half this place is made up of transplanted northerners, active and ex-military, retirees, snowbirds, and last week I met an astronaut and an ocean researcher within hours of each other. And *now*, I'm talking with a lady P.I. Life is rich, isn't it?"

What a paradox this man was, Diane thought. He was laid-back here with her at the moment, yet he owned the reputation of being a perfectionist when it came to rigorous rehearsals and water performances. No room for chatty fluff between segments or superfluous moves in the water. Flawless performances didn't happen otherwise.

"It's interesting, to say the least," Diane replied. *And I might be talking to a murderer* zoomed through her mind.

The scotches arrived, and Sam didn't move one toward her. "Put these on my tab," he instructed the server, whose name Diane would probably never learn. While Sam wet his whistle, she relaxed. Talking and swallowing at the same time were unlikely. She needed Sam to talk.

So, until then, she wondered how anyone went through their work life being nameless. It could be handy, at times, she supposed. But a name rooted a person, could even help clinch their destiny or legacy. Like Marilyn, or Zorro, or Pink. Diane got a wild hare to guess the server girl's name. Christy? That was it. Christy.

Diane adjusted the silver bracelet on her arm as Sam finished his second shot.

"Let's talk more," she said, "about Mermaid Nerissa closer to the time of her death."

Sam's expression sobered, despite his choice of refreshment. "I tell you what. Just between you and me, about a week before her last performance, I noticed her moves were off in the triple twist. I mentioned it to her...*gently*...*because it's my job*, and she started to cry."

Diane fanned away wayward strands of hair from her face. "What'd you do then?"

"She was no stage baby, but I *gently* asked her what's wrong. And she just shook her head and clammed up. Then on another day she became dizzy."

"Dizzy? As in falling-over dizzy?"

"More like sliding out of the clamshell on her ass dizzy."

Diane pulled herself to the front edge of the chair. "Isn't that dangerous underwater?"

"Way! Way more than I can say. We all get physical exams every year, and her last one checked out fine. I put Hannah on standby in case this got worse. But Nerissa came through with flying colors during our final dress rehearsal and, except for almost missing that cue near the end of the last show, our star mermaid was totally on target.

"By then, I blew off all her moods, fits, and misses, and Hannah swam her regular bit. She did a good job. Then, not long after Nerissa took her final underwater bow, she'd died. Outside of the tank! She was *gone*." His voice cracked. "There'll never be another Mermaid Nerissa show."

Sam's intensity bombarded her. She gripped her pen tighter. "Regarding delayed cues, do you think she had a lapse in focus?"

"Maybe. I chalked it up to pre-performance pressure or not drinking enough water that day. We also work at keeping hydrated. We live in Florida, you know. The Summer Splash Bash is a huge event for us. It messes with our daily routines and breaks. Forgive the saying, but it's do-or-die time. Either the show works and fireworks are set off, or it fails and word gets out. I can guarantee you that Apollo expects only one outcome in the end: Success." Sam pushed aside the empty glasses. "Well, he got it that night for damned sure. He'd even given us a bonus."

"Hmm, that was generous of him."

Sam rubbed his thumb over a knuckle. "Then all hell broke loose. Neptune's Grotto was closed for ten days. Services for Nerissa were held on the beach. Her family came. Her grandmother is one of our regular patrons. Several people offered eulogies.

"Nerissa's boyfriend almost lost it, and we had to get the medics out here because Chef Eric accidentally nicked his wrist with a carving knife. Worst ten days here ever. So, when you're talking to us around here, don't be surprised if we want to avoid the topic."

Diane leaned toward him. "Fortunately, it's been the contrary. But I feel your pain."

The choreographer grew sullen. "All I can say, I lost my chance to work with one of the most talented, smart, and creative women in this industry. No matter how much I work with Hannah, she'll never reach Nerissa's level. But Apollo's happy, and that's what matters most."

He lifted an empty glass toward the server.

"The same?" the girl asked as she approached.

"Please, Christy," he said, and she returned quickly with one. Sam raised it toward Diane, "Cheers, and just *catch* the lunatic, will you?"

Thirteen

Whose Idea?

Diane returned to her office an hour after meeting with Sam Lock. His voice resonated in her ears, and his intensity sapped her energy. She walked into her case room and tacked the two postcards she'd purchased to the board. Her collection of items was growing.

The same thing was true for her handwritten facts and questions on the white board next to it. Still, too many questions stared back at Diane. Undeniably, they tested her panache for sleuthing.

The items were in no particular order, despite how much she loathed chaos. In Nerissa's case, there was something amiss. Something was out of order. Cover-ups and lies helped.

Her case To Do list had shortened. She reviewed the list of the ground she'd covered. She then frowned with concern. The keen partnership existing between her fact finding efforts and trusting her sharp intuition wobbled. Clearly, her strong hunch system was faltering. She had little more of a clue about who killed Mermaid Nerissa than she did a week ago.

That worried her. Her business was to seek facts, sift, and solve. The seeking and gathering part was at a furor. The sifting and solving parts suffered. Her thoughts turned dark. Whose idea was this, anyway? threatened to be asked. She'd failed at delivering children for her and Tom to rear and love. She *couldn't* fail at this, too.

In the quiet, Diane picked up the erasable red felt-tip marker resting on the tray and twisted off the top. Red lines soon streaked through the items she'd done today. She reattached the cap and left the room for the kitchen.

After pouring herself ice water, Diane returned to her office, shucked off her shoes, and sank into the comfy stuffed chintz-covered chair in front of her desk. Glancing at her knitting basket parked on the front corner of her desk, she stretched and pulled it to herself. The soft yarn on her fingers comforted and inspired her as she dug gleaming, empty Clarice out from her hiding place and laid her on the arm of the chair. So far, she never had to point her pistol at anyone, let alone use her. Except for once a month when she went with Tom for practice shooting.

Diane took up the pair of US size nine bamboo needles and pulled off their pink guards. For Kitty, doing jigsaw puzzles relaxed her, but Diane derived relaxation from mastering patterns like cable, basket weave, stockinet, and others. While knitting scarves, she let her mind roam freely and simultaneously created something useful and pretty. Even Tom found them attractive. An hour passed of knit one, purl one, and the last thing Diane saw was a dropped stitch…

When she opened her eyes next, Tom was standing over her.

"Ahh, so this is where you are?" he asked, sounding put off. "I've been trying to reach you. Kitty was taken over to St. Vincent's Hospital, and she wanted you to know."

Diane dropped her knitting and rose from the chair. "What's wrong with her?"

"She fell. She has a severely bruised patella. We can go see her in the morning."

Relieved it wasn't worse, Diane leaned against him, and he wrapped his arms around her. "Tom, I know this case is all you hear from me lately, but my head's buzzing again with new things. Like, how would a master chef accidentally nick himself at the wrist with a carving knife? And why was Chelsea giving him money?"

"Oh yes, the life of an investigator."

"Also, I still have a little matter of a foreign substance present in her wound. Between checking on this and meeting Chelsea's best friend, my days need to be longer. Then there's the mess with my competition, who's a total fake and a blackmailer. When will he turn up next? Detective Brooks is looking funny at Eric the chef because he owed Chelsea money and never said so. Her choreographer reported she was slipping up in technical moves. Finally, Chelsea was definitely going through something troublesome, but nobody knew what, not even her boyfriend." She shook a little and urgency riddled her voice.

Tom looked down at her and must've read the signals. "When did you eat last?"

She thought back. "Breakfast."

His voice deepened. "You need to practice more self-compassion. How're you going to help others without taking care of yourself?" He steered her toward the door. "Let's get home, clean up, and go to One Ocean for dinner."

Diane re-gathered her knitting, laid it in the wicker basket, and cradled Clarice deep inside. "You're on."

Fourteen

Kitty Took a Spill

The next morning, Diane and Tom arrived in Kitty's room just after she'd come back from radiology for more X-rays. She wore a hospital print gown and covered her shoulders with a lightweight, hand-crocheted sweater. Her hair, as usual, was neatly coiffed and her eyes flickered with worry.

"It was the silliest thing," Kitty fretted. "I was watering the oleander, and I tripped on the flagstone. Now I'm here, and it looks like I'll be hobbling along with a walker until this gets better. But I should be out of here by my birthday on Friday."

Tom handed her flowers. "You're going to be okay, Lady Kitty."

Diane seconded his sentiment. "I don't have a green thumb, but I'll water plants for you."

Kitty brightened. "You're too good to me."

"Mutual," Diane said and gave her a hug.

"Could you bring me my jacket?" she asked Diane and nodded at a cupboard across the room. "There's something in the pocket I want to give you."

Diane opened the door, pulled a tan jacket from the hook inside, and brought it to her. Kitty pulled out a pink envelope and gave it to Diane. "This is a thank you note to Hannah. I hope you'll give it to her on your next visit to Blue Wave. I'd written it just before my swan dive on the patio."

Diane slipped it into her bag. "I'm going down there tomorrow. There are a few more things I want to check."

Pleased, Kitty leaned back and rested her head on the pillow. "Give Apollo my regards, if you should see him, too." She covered a yawn with her hand. "Excuse me, that pain pill they gave me is making me sleepy."

Diane and Tom exchanged relieved glances. "We'll be on our way for now," Diane said.

Kitty smiled. "Thanks for help with the watering. The hose is on the back patio. When I get home and am back to myself, I'll bake you two a pie."

Diane squeezed her hand. "There, there. No need for that."

Kitty squeezed back. "On your way out, would you please tell the nurses I don't want any more company?"

"Sure, we can do that," Tom said.

"Just before I went to radiology, a man came to see me about Chelsea. He looked kind of grubby, but since he's an investigator, I'll let it slide. He's doing his job, and I'm grateful to anyone who can help find who murdered my granddaughter."

Diane stiffened. "An investigator?"

Tom stepped closer. "Who was he, Kitty?"

She closed her eyes and murmured, "I don't remember…his card's there on the windowsill. See you soon." And she was out for the count.

Thirty-five minutes later, Diane met Detective Brooks in the hospital lobby. She made the customary introductions, and Tom and he shook hands.

"I'm glad you called," Brooks said, eyeing the card she'd handed him. "How long ago was he here?"

"An hour or more now."

He ran his hand through his hair over his ear. "Is your client awake, available to talk?"

"I'm sorry to say she's not. Meds are doing their good thing for her."

He grimaced and snapped the card with his thumb and forefinger.

"It says here his name is Sol Foster and now with a Sanford address. This creep's changing identities like we do our clothes. But his *investigation* days are numbered. Keep me posted, Ms. Phipps."

Diane raised her hand. "I do have a question. You'd mentioned that Chelsea Graham had paid money to Eric Jameson. Can you expand on that?"

Brooks slipped his hand into his pocket. "Not with much. Her bank records showed that two months before she died she'd written him a check for three thousand five hundred dollars. On the note line on the front of the check, she'd written LOAN."

Diane side-glanced Tom. He'd stepped away to pick up a newspaper from the rack near a group of lobby chairs. "Was she paying off a loan she'd gotten from him, or was she giving him a loan?"

"Word is she'd given him one."

"And there was no deposit in that amount listed later for it?"

"Nope," Brooks said. "After she died, her account was frozen and eventually closed."

Diane crinkled her nose. "So it's possible the loan was never repaid to her."

"I'd say it's probable."

"Thanks."

Tom arrived back at her side. Detective Brooks gestured toward Tom's injured hand.

"What happened there?" Brooks asked casually.

Tom tossed him a quick nod. "Work injury."

They exchanged understanding glances. "Well, take it easy. Both of you."

Diane and he said their goodbyes, and she left the hospital with her hand tucked into Tom's crooked arm. "He's a good guy," she said as they left through the front doors.

The breeze lifted the tails of her turquoise shirt.

"Detective Brooks likes baseball," Tom commented.

Diane nudged him with her elbow. "How d'you know that?"

"By his handshake. He used to play ball. A pitcher, is my bet."

Suddenly, she remembered the Jacksonville Jumbo Shrimp tickets on his desk during her last visit with him at headquarters. "You're incredible."

He winked. "Nope, he has a strong grip, and he approached our shake with a modified arc. After the grasp, he followed through with an overhand turn."

Diane slowed to a stop. "Is there anything you can't figure out?"

Her husband gave her a simple, "Yes. How to keep people from killing each other. I know this mermaid case has you all torqued up. But the answers will come, my dear. Keep the faith."

She squeezed his hand.

"Look at things from all angles," he reminded, "and ask the right questions."

Fifteen

One Swan, Please

The next day, Diane walked into the kitchen at Blue Wave, and Chef Eric met her at the door with a rope of garlic in his hand. "Hi, Ms. Phipps. You like us so much you couldn't keep away?" he asked jovially.

She stepped toward him. "Could be something like that," she bantered back. "I need to check on having an ice sculpture made, please. A swan, small and tasteful, if you can squeeze it into your schedule?"

Chef Eric smiled and tossed the garlic rope onto a stainless steel counter. Salad makers, cooks, and dishwashers in training filled the room. "I'm sure I can. Come with me to my office." That meant the ice room, and this time Diane was wearing jeans and a knit top, socks, and shoes. "What's the occasion, and when do you need it?" he asked as they donned the reefers and entered the frigid room.

"Friday afternoon for a birthday party for Mermaid Nerissa's grandmother."

Chef Eric beamed. "What's the color scheme?"

She leveled her gaze on him and cleared her throat. "The color of money. Green."

Chef Eric turned toward her. His smile was fading. "That's different, but green is nature's color, and we can work with it." He put his finger on his bottom lip. "Except there are many shades of green, so I'll need a little—"

"Chef Eric, I'm also here about another matter."

He raised an eyebrow. "And what is it?"

Her breath fogged in front of her. "Well, I've learned that Mermaid Nerissa loaned you a tidy sum of money, and when we met earlier, it never came up. I just thought you'd like to share with me why you needed three thousand five hundred dollars…and if you were able to pay it back before she died."

There, it was out in the open, like dirty laundry hanging on a line in a back alley. Diane widened her stance and clasped her hands in front of her.

Chef Eric sucked in a breath and blew it out hurriedly. "What? Are you a debt collector now?" He didn't wait for her reply. "Yes, I borrowed money from her, and it was a private matter, and it *still* needs to be a private matter. Now, do you really want an ice sculpture?"

Diane narrowed the gap between them. His facial expression looked tortured. "I do, and I also need you to be ultra-straight with me. You should have nothing to worry about, Chef Eric. But it's a curious factor that Detective Brooks has uncovered, and both of us like to have all the pieces of a murder puzzle to put together so none of them are missing at the end. Right now I'm juggling a lot of pieces."

"And I'm an irregular one?" he asked lightly. "I've occasionally liked boys, I admit."

"Never mind."

She supposed it was her gentler tone of voice that encouraged Chef Eric to ease up. "Fine, we'll talk. Come over to the design table and I'll show you some drawing samples of swans. Is this for a centerpiece on a table?"

Diane confirmed that with a shiver and followed him. "Will you make it all shimmery?"

"That's no problem either. I can infuse it with my iridescent diamond dust."

She checked the drawings and picked one.

"Excellent choice," he said. "I have a two-piece mold right here for that size." He began writing an order for her.

"Thank you," she said as he finished.

Chef Eric attached it to a bulletin board and asked, "Would you like a coffee?"

Diane fought the urge to accept, but failed. "I could use one, yes."

He poured her one in a thermal mug. "C'mon, let's walk."

"Where?" she asked after taking a sip.

"Right here. We make a big circle; keeps us moving, and our body heats up."

Diane saw the logic and fell into step with him. "So, Chef Eric, what's all this about a loan? And I can't stick here very long; I'm freezing. So could you just give me the details, and if it's all on the level, I'll see you Friday when you deliver the sculpture."

He looked at her with compassion. "This is to go nowhere. If Apollo gets wind of it, your swan will be the last sculpture I'll make for Blue Wave. He surrounds himself with people he believes are smarter than usual. I made a dumb move that involved another employee. I'll be out of here on my ear."

Diane widened her eyes. "*What* could he object to about you?"

"Like I'd said when we last met, Apollo employs people with clean records. He won't tolerate shenanigans. Tips are even monitored with a year-end tally for taxes."

Diane passed the lion sculpture that was coming along nicely.

"Are you saying you have a record?" If so, it didn't come up in the police reports.

Chef Eric slowed his pace. "No, I don't, but I have a…habit."

"Drugs?"

"Feels like it, but no. You see, I *like* to make my money grow. Aggressively. I had bought stocks, and they unexpectedly tanked fast. That got me into deep trouble with the people who loaned me the money to buy them." He lowered his gaze for a few seconds. "Their next stop was collections and wage garnishment. I would've been up the creek if Apollo found out. So I reached out to some friends and asked for help. Mermaid Nerissa was one of them."

Diane thought ahead. "Did that make you nervous? I mean, she could've let it slip around work. Even whoever loaned you the investment funds could've spilled the beans if they didn't like how you took care of your debt to them."

Diane pressed her lips together and gave him a minute to regroup.

Chef Eric resumed, "I would've crossed that bridge if, or when, I came to it."

"Well, you're still here. That says a lot."

Chef Eric drank from his mug and lifted it her direction. "I took on some sculpting jobs on the side, and I've paid them all back. I still have Nerissa's money, and I've been trying to think of a way to honor her with it."

Diane finished the coffee and set the mug down on the workbench they passed. This walking thing didn't work as well as it should, she decided. She flapped her arms at her sides like penguin wings. "I have to say this, you're a lucky soul. Forget using green for the sculpted swan. Let's have a graceful, clear, sparkly, shimmery version instead."

He led her to the door and opened it for them. Spilling out into the kitchen, Diane took off the parka and greeted the warmth.

"Honestly, I don't know *how* people live in Montana and North Dakota."

"They wear bison hide parkas and probably eat hardy stew by a big roaring fire."

His answer made sense. "That's because you're part polar bear and foodie."

"Thanks for your sculpture order, Ms. Phipps."

She turned to him. "Thanks for our talk, Chef Eric."

As she turned around, she felt his gaze boring into her back. She'd pushed his buttons for sure, but none of them had set off blazing fireworks.

Next, Diane took the passageway behind the show tank, hoping to catch Hannah in the mermaids' dressing room. Again, she found the door ajar and stepped inside the room. The clock showed 1:30, and Diane pulled Kitty's thank you note from her bag and set it on the vanity in front of the center mirror. Turning to go, she heard steps coming down the passageway. She exited the room just as a rotund woman with fiery red hair bustled toward her.

She pushed a cart capped with a silver and lavender mermaid tail. "Hi, miss, Can I help you?" She steered it into the dressing room and parked it off to the side.

Diane eyed her with wonder. A blue streak meandered down one side of her hair and the other side was pushed up and held in place with a sparkly clip. A sea star, to be exact.

"I think I have it, and I'm Diane, a private investigator working on the Mermaid Nerissa case. I just left a note for Hannah. I met her here recently."

The woman dropped an oversized bag on the floor. "I'm Rosa Delacroix, costume mistress for the show. Hannah's off today, and she better not be eating effing cheeseburgers. I've had to have two tails remolded for her in the last three weeks. She's putting on weight." She sneezed and used a tissue.

"Bless you," Diane said, unable to look away from her colorful skirt and loose shirt and rows and rows of beads resting on her ample chest. "So Hannah's keeping you busy?"

Arms akimbo, Rosa fisted her hands at her waist. "Ha! Busy in more ways than one. Hannah's not as self-disciplined as Mermaid Nerissa. She craves the spotlight and is a free spirit and all that malarkey. She wanted to tattoo her arms, but that got a resounding 'No!' from Apollo. Last week I caught her making out in here with *another* fan."

"Another fan?"

Rosa rolled her eyes. "Not the first. She embarrassed Nerissa silly when she found Hannah with a guy in her chair."

Reeling from the imagery, Diane raised her fingers to her temples. *Put it into perspective,* her inner voice said. "I'd say it's a good thing Apollo hasn't heard about that."

"Not yet, anyway. He'd be having serious words with her. But Hannah's the big star now, so Mr. Clean wouldn't cut her off. Now, I sure don't tell her that part, mind you. She needs *something* to keep her on the beam." She narrowed her eyes and almost whispered, "Still, stardom comes with perks."

Diane blinked at the underhanded tip. "For some at Blue Wave, but not all?"

"You're right. Most of us couldn't get away with things she does." She snorted. "Of course I wouldn't want to; I'm thirty-six. All that said, Hannah is still an eager learner. She likes to try new techniques and moves in the show, and that keeps her on the cutting edge and Sam happy."

Diane's phone rang. She pulled it from the pocket and checked the screen. "Ah, do you mind if I take this?"

Rosa waved both hands at her. "You go ahead, missy. Business is business."

"Hello, Jennifer," Diane said. "Thanks for calling me back. Yes, it's about Chelsea. Good, I'll meet you tomorrow at ten at Fort Caroline. Bye for now."

Diane hung up, thanked Rosa for her time, and left Blue Wave with a lot more than she had walked in with. Chef Eric confirmed Chelsea had given him money as a favor, and her time with Rosa revealed Hannah was a handful.

Sixteen

Best Friends Forever

At 9:45 the next morning, Diane drove through the modest entrance to the Fort Caroline National Memorial, passed the National Park Service sign, and left her car in the lot. Tall, old live oaks and palms draped with Spanish moss gave her an instant view of "Old Florida." She walked past the right side of the visitor center building and took the curved lane leading up a rise to the open pavilion situated by the magnolia and holly trees. She spotted Jennifer McCall waiting for her at one of the picnic tables.

Wearing olive pants and a sleeveless white shirt, Jennifer rose from the bench. Diane exchanged a polite handshake with her. The girl's large hazel eyes were well-spaced. Her full smile was bright, and she weighed maybe one hundred thirty-five pounds. A Cousteau Marine Institute Lab cap covered her smooth brunette hair, and she exuded good health.

"Thank you for meeting with me here," Chelsea's best friend said. "It's off the beaten path from the city, and we get a great view of the river. Chelsea and I would come here with picnic lunches, and we'd look for gopher tortoises and burrow owls." Her voice shook. "We're into…rather, we were into nature and had studied together."

Diane handed her a Starbucks latte. "I know this is tough. Would you like to sit or walk?"

"Walking's better." Jennifer accepted the drink and strung a small bag over her shoulder. Diane fell into step with her as they made their way over the grass to the lookout platform and benches behind the visitor center. "Would you like to visit the Fort?" she asked Diane off-handedly. "We can go inside and make our donation and meet the park ranger on duty. They all know my dad."

At the moment, Diane was taking in the panoramic view of the wide St. Johns River.

"Maybe next time?" she answered. This was a part of Florida she'd not seen yet but had caught references from locals. Although it was Timicuan, the French and Spanish history about it was barbaric and sad. Still, Tom would enjoy exploring there someday. Clouds overhead darkened the water and a breeze kicked up whitecaps.

Jennifer slowed and set her coffee on top of a railing. "I miss Chelsea so much. She was like a sister to me."

"Her Grandma Kitty told me you were close friends."

"Chelsea and I had graduated together. Then she went on her way with professional swimming, and I went on my own. We didn't get to see each other much, but we'd texted. I'd accepted a position at the Institute, which keeps me here and further south."

"Cousteau Marine Lab? Sounds interesting."

"For now, I help sick sea turtles get better and monitor their nests on the beaches during mating season, May through October. Chelsea would come volunteer every once in a while." She stopped for another sip of coffee. "Are these the things you want to know about her?"

Diane smiled. "I like knowing everything about Chelsea. She was different and vibrant."

"*And she never deserved to die.*" Jennifer's bottom lip quivered.

Diane moved closer to her. "You're right," she said gently. "I'd like to know if she had an enemy. Maybe she'd unwittingly stepped on someone's toes? Also, I'm hearing that just before her death her mood had changed. She had minor difficulty with some of the moves she performed well. So, if she shared any secrets with you about something going wrong, I need to know because they might be very important."

Diane's plea hung in the breeze while Jennifer raised her chin.

In a low tone she said, "Yes, something was up. Chelsea wanted to leave Blue Wave and come to work with us at the lab. She had the education and credentials. We'd made a pinky swear about this, and I'm not a promise breaker."

Diane's breath rushed from her chest. "Leave her career?" It took her a moment to ask the next one. "Why?"

"I don't know what got it all started," Jennifer said. "Except that she was having stress headaches. But who doesn't?" She held her cup with both hands. "Mr. Redstone had wanted her to add another show to her day. That would've cut deeply into her free time, and she and Luke were going to get married…but few people knew that. Anyway, she was so driven to do the Summer Splash Bash performances perfectly. Anything less would've thrown her into a Southern tizzy fit."

Diane nodded with concern. "Were you at the event?"

"I saw her first performance at seven and then had to leave. I have a fiancé, too."

"Sure. Everyone raves about her performances that night. Do you think she wanted them to be her swan song shows?"

Jennifer crossed her arms and looked at her intently. "Yes, I do. And it's perceptive of you to consider that." Her eyes shone with respect. "My boss called her two days before the show and offered her a position to start work in August. We'd also been doing studies with certain mollusks—oysters—in the estuary along A1A. She accepted, and the only thing left to do was negotiate her salary. She'd planned to meet with Apollo the day after the show to give him her notice. She told me she simply wanted to do something more meaningful than entertaining people. She wanted to return to her field of study for the sake of marine life conservation."

Diane kicked a leaf aside with her foot. "You do know how to keep secrets."

"I'm sure *you* do, too," Jennifer quipped with a laugh.

"It comes with the territory." Finishing her latte, Diane tossed the cup in a trash receptacle. "Now, I still wonder if Chelsea ever complained about anyone at work."

Jennifer turned and looked out at the water. "Not really. She toughed it out when problems came along and didn't complain much. But there was one time when something weird came up. It was close to her last show. It has always bothered me."

Diane leaned in for more details. Her visit had yielded gold nuggets. But she still lacked that gut-level hunch surety that flared when she was dead on the mark. "Tell me about what happened."

Chelsea's friend raised her hand. "Do you mind if we walk some more?"

Diane would've walked to St. Augustine with her. "Not at all. I'm in no hurry."

Jennifer discarded her empty cup and began walking around to the front of the building.

"Chelsea called me one day and wanted to have lunch. I was able to make it happen, so we met at Chili's close to the lab. Her newest promo photos had arrived the day before, and she'd found the envelope on her vanity in the dressing room. When she opened it, she found the pictures ripped apart and stuffed back into the envelope." Jennifer huffed. "Can you imagine someone doing that?"

Diane winced. "Not anyone who liked her much, that's for sure."

Jennifer pulled her bag from her shoulder. "She brought one of the less damaged photos with her, and she gave it to me."

"Do you still have it?"

"I do." Opening her bag, Jennifer pulled out a small envelope. She lifted the flap and dropped four pieces into her palm. "Even though it's torn, I carry it with me."

Diane switched her gaze from the pieces back to Jennifer. "This is new evidence."

Jennifer hesitated. "It's the last thing Chelsea gave me."

Diane patted the back of Jennifer's hand. "It's important. You'll have made a worthy contribution to the investigation of the murder of Chelsea Graham."

Jennifer straightened her spine. "Then, keep it, please. Even if it's forever."

Diane thanked her as Chelsea's friend slipped them back into the envelope.

Diane's mind raced while she tucked it into her bag. Things just didn't add up. How could Chelsea, who got along so well and was so liked, take such a nasty turn? Worse, end up *dead?* While she mused, faces of all the people she'd interviewed streamed before her mind's eye. Rolling her fingers on the table top, she said, "Someone's sure talking up a good game, because *someone* has a lot to hide."

Jennifer sighed and wrapped her arms around herself. "And I sincerely hope you'll find out who. It'd be for Chelsea's sake and for those of us who really did care about her."

Diane walked with her to the parking lot. "I do have two more questions," she said. "Has anyone else other than Detective Brooks or me visited with you about Chelsea?"

Jennifer pulled her car keys out of her bag. "No, am I to expect that?"

"Not really, but if they do, can you give me call?"

"I will. But in about two weeks I'm going on vacation. What's your other question?"

Diane opened her car door. "Did Chelsea keep a journal or a diary?"

Jennifer shook her head back and forth. "Nah, we grew out of that stuff after college."

Diane waved and watched Jennifer drive away from the lot. She sat in her car and pulled her notebook from her bag. Quickly, she wrote on the pages so as not to forget one tidbit of information.

She arrived at her office a while later and took a headache tablet. The palm trees were shedding their seeds, and maybe an allergy to them was the cause. Whatever, she was looking ahead to a quiet but working evening. She'd covered good ground so far in this case and now had met all the principals in Chelsea Graham's life, except for Merman Owen and making a call to her parents.

On the way home, Diane stopped at the sheriff's office. Detective Brooks was at his desk wearing a ball cap and sunglasses. "Don't say a word." He glowered. "The captain ordered me to go to a game. He says my eyes look like roadmaps and my disposition is in the toilet. He doesn't want a burnout on his team. I'm driving over to the stadium to catch the Jumbo Shrimp play the Mavericks at seven-o-five. But I can see you're busting at the seams about something, Ms. Phipps. So *what* is it, please?"

Diane raised her chin. Personally, she'd hate to see bags form under Brooks' eyes. She looked around the room, noting it was less busy than the last time she was there. "Well, relaxation does wonders, so enjoy."

He frowned. "I don't have time for games," he railed and tossed a wad of paper into a basket.

She pressed. "Why not do something closer to home?"

"What would that be? Woodworking?"

Diane shrugged. "If it suits you, or have you tried knitting?"

Brooks glared at her.

"A lot of guys knit," she said unfazed. "Football players. Concert pianists. It's comforting to move yarn around in a rhythm from needle to needle and end up with a usable item."

The detective narrowed his eyes. "I take it you knit?"

"I do."

"WHY?" He threw his hands up in the air. "We live in HOT-damn FLORIDA!"

Diane settled a calm gaze on him. "Tom and I have relatives and friends in cool climates. Hand-knitted scarves are good holiday gifts from the heart."

Beau Brooks scratched an eyebrow with his middle finger. "My sister lives in Iowa. I send her gift cards. Now, could we get on with why you're here to share your cheeriness with me?"

A smile teased the corner of his lips, hinting that his bark was worse than his bite. She had every confidence that the break at the ball park would put him on track. Especially since Tom believed he was connected to baseball. *Once a player, always a player?* crossed her mind. Along with it came, *look at things from all angles,* and *ask the right questions.* Tom made her proud.

"Yes, of course." Diane opened her bag and presented the small envelope Jennifer had given her with Chelsea's photo inside.

He held it up, turned it over a couple times, and waited for her to continue.

"Chelsea's best friend Jennifer gave this to me today. It's a headshot of Mermaid Nerissa they'd used for publicity."

He crooked an eyebrow and interest sparked in his eyes. "She was a looker."

"I thought you'd want it." She relayed what Jennifer had told her about the situation.

He lifted the envelope flap and peered inside. "Good work, Ms. Phipps." Half turning in his chair, he opened a desk drawer and pulled out a plastic evidence bag. He slipped the envelope inside and zipped the top shut. "I'll run the pieces through ID for prints."

Diane beamed and rose from the chair. "I was hoping so. I'll run along now."

Brooks raised his hand for her to wait. "Listen, I've been wondering about something, if you have a minute?"

She settled on the chair edge and held her purse on top of her knees. "What have you been wondering about, Detective Brooks?"

He gave her a look. "It's a long shot, but have you thought about rejoining the force?"

Diane stilled. "You mean like here?"

Brooks nodded. "We're not chopped liver."

"No, you're not," she said, meaning it. "But I enjoy making my own day and taking the risks and getting to the bottom of things and serving justice doing it. On my own. But thank you for thinking of me. I take it as a compliment."

The detective raised a finger at her. "You should. There's some promising talk of expanding our team in the fall. You're on my wish list of possible candidates."

Diane couldn't hide the rush of pride that must've colored her cheeks. "I haven't solved the mermaid case. So my credentials aren't established, but I do thank you."

Brooks got up from his chair. "I understand…more than you'll know." He waved the evidence bag back and forth in front of her. "Thanks for this…and happy knitting."

Diane soon left the building and, in a haze, drove by fluffy magenta crepe myrtle trees and through five o'clock traffic. She looked forward to musing over her case board for a while. Around seven, she'd go home and take a bubble bath. After eating soup with

Tom, she could settle at the table, re-assemble a mini-crime board in front of her, and review her notes. She also would look again at Kitty's pictures and finally snuggle with Tom under the covers.

He'd been patient lately, despite how he'd had to unexpectedly pull the plug from his own work. The amount of his days at home were dwindling. Soon he'd repack and leave for a new assignment. But between now and then, they would celebrate Kitty's birthday.

Seventeen

The Merman

The numbers on the digital clock on the microwave in Diane's kitchen flipped to two a.m. Her pajama bottoms hugged her legs as she sat crossed-legged on a chair. Often she did her best thinking like this, and Lord knew she needed to concentrate…in comfort. While Tom slept, she arranged the photos she'd stripped from her office case board in front of her on the table. She had one for each person she had interviewed. Before she'd come home, she also had scratched off more items from her lengthy To Do list.

The few that remained ended with: Solve this case!

Diane was down to the wire. Kitty needed a shot of good news, and Detective Brooks was anticipating updates. So far, she'd invested the best of her sleuthing self to uncover motives and identify Chelsea's killer. She had gone at it with her heart, too.

Truthfully, Diane began to feel as if she *owned* this case. But could she catch the brass ring? For sure, she needed something big, bold, and conclusive to sprout and take root. Every time a piece or element fell into place—sometimes with a hardy plunk, and others drifted into view like a ship in the mist—the hint of victory spurred her on to intrepidly find the next.

Sitting with the company of coffee, notes, photos, and hope, Diane summoned her logic and senses to help. Like people, cases had personalities. They had their good and bad hair days, quirks, and twists. They shaped her schedule and her thinking. Tom was so right, too. *She needed to keep the faith.*

She sighted each photo arranged in alphabetical order and moved them into tiers like a pyramid with Chelsea's picture at the peak. It struck her as an amazing assortment of folks who were close to the victim in her work world and otherwise.

A resort owner, two co-swimmers, a choreographer, her boyfriend, a wardrobe mistress, a chef and ice sculptor, a bartender, her best friend, and her disillusioned grandmother all had made time to talk with Diane. She scrutinized each one, looking for a hint of malice in their eyes. However, none of the images talked to her enough.

By three a.m. Diane leaned back in the chair and sleepily held Kitty's pictures in her palm. She flipped one over the other, slowed the rhythm, and raised her eyebrows. Leaning forward, she pulled the lamp closer and laid two photos side-by-side on the table and compared them.

Diane's heart thumped. She slid her focus to the victim's beautiful face and whispered, "Oh dear, Chelsea. What happened here? How did I miss this?"

~ * ~

Diane caught up with Merman Owen Wagner at the Seascape Gym in Neptune Beach. He looked pretty much the same as he did in the marquis photos she'd seen at Blue Wave. Chelsea's death had brought about many changes. One major one was that Owen had left the Blue Wave, and that alone caused a stir. Three weeks later, he'd turned up in Savannah, Georgia, working as a host at Paula Deen's restaurant. Up until last month, that was.

Why he left and decided to come back to beach life interested Diane. But the cops didn't care much about any of it. He hadn't gone missing the night of Chelsea's murder, only after the fact. Everyone had chalked up his leaving to how much he had hated working without her. They were a perfect match under water. Apparently, they were better than any ice skating pair or ballet partners. So, when she died, it had seemed that part of him did, too.

With his and everyone else's alibi intact, Diane considered the possibility that someone had arranged for her murder, not done it personally. So from that view, every person she interviewed could've been the culprit. Including Owen, who was bench pressing two hundred fifty pounds of weights.

"I figured you'd turn up eventually," he said, squinting up at her.

Diane smiled. "Why's that?"

"Eric called me that you're making the rounds. Said you're a good dresser for being a gumshoe. You have a Gucci bag. I bought my mom one for Christmas."

"Eric say anything else?"

"Uh-huh. That you have a lot of *chutzpah*. He's right. No lady I know walks into this part of the gym."

She could believe it. It smelled like old socks. She also had to be careful where she swept her gaze. She wasn't a fan of hairy armpits and groaning jocks. Also, male anatomy had a way of peeking out from loose shorts.

"D'you have a minute?"

He cradled the bar with a loud clank and sat up. Sweat soaked the front of his tank top. His shoulders and face glistened. Diane handed him the white towel from the courtesy carousel.

He nodded and mopped his face. "Let's go to the Smoothie Bar." He threw on an Adidas wind breaker and left it unzipped.

She followed him out the double swinging doors and down a short hall to an open health food courtyard. "Pick a spot, any spot," he said. "You up for a Heart Throb?"

She gazed blankly at him.

"That'd be carrots, kale, crushed pineapple," he injected, "and a double shot of whey protein."

"I just need water," she said, choosing a round table by a window.

He returned with a bottle of water and a tall plastic cup with a thick carrot reaching for the sky from the center and its shaggy top draping over the lip.

"Water's free."

"Nice."

He sat opposite her. "This is my lunch and dinner," he explained as he pulled an oversized straw from a dispenser and jammed it into the drink.

"Really?"

"I wouldn't lie to you."

"Good. I've got some questions."

She waited for him to finish his first pull. It made her wonder how he could suck for so long without taking a breath. Then, she remembered he'd been a merman.

He finished and leaned back into the chair. Casually, he lifted a finger for her to begin.

"I'm curious why you left Blue Wave and the best job you probably ever had?"

"Because with Chelsea it was the best job I'd *ever* have. When she was gone, I was virtually done. Hannah is a spoiled diva. She's in the game for herself—not teamwork or for the art of it, that's for damn sure."

Made sense. "Why'd you go to Savannah?"

"Ava left to be up there with her sick mother and wanted me to come. So I drove up right after Chelsea's funeral. I also found temporary work. Not to run away from anything—like murder—for crying out loud."

A dark shadow passed through his eyes, and he fell silent. Diane made notes.

"Not only that," he erupted, "it would've been impossible for me to work with the Hart woman very long. She can't hold still in the water, doesn't hold her breath for more than three effing minutes, but she claims it's for four and a half. She won't follow a script. What good is that?" He grimaced. "I was only as good as the star mermaid Everything—the story, my role and moves—revolved around her."

Diane put down her pen. "You seem frustrated, angry, Owen."

He twirled his thumbs. "Ha. I do?" His tone wore sarcasm like a coat. "Someone had killed the best days of my thirty-four year life."

"It was going to change anyway, and you knew it. She was marrying Luke."

He didn't flinch. "Married women can still swim."

"But then Chelsea couldn't be your wife. And you loved her."

"Yes, ma'am, I did. From first sight."

"Was it mutual?"

"Nope. We went out twice, but—"

"No spark from her for you?"

"I'd hope it would hit over time." He suddenly looked lost.

She cleared her throat. "Unrequited love is—"

"As lousy as it gets."

Diane drank some water. "Must've made you sad to know you couldn't have her."

"Deeply sad, but not mad. It can still get me down if I think about it too much."

"Shame. So you had someone kill her?"

He laughed outright. "Really? Oh my God, I don't know the right people for that. Back then I also would've tried to hate her after she hooked up with Talbot. I would've failed. Love meant I wanted her to be happy. Not dead." He plucked the carrot from the smoothie, chomped off the pointy tip and chewed. Bobbing what was left of the carrot at Diane, he added, "And I know you're trying to solve this case and will earn stars for it. But I'm not your dream come true, Ms. Phipps."

She gave Owen a long apprising look. Not one nervous gesture. No avoidance of eye contact. More than that, her trusted gut told her flat out this guy wasn't the killer.

"Nope, you're not."

He sighed. "I'm glad we agree."

"Any idea about what happened?" she ventured.

He shook his head. "Not a clue, sorry. But one person does."

"Exactly. The one who stabbed her in the neck."

Eighteen

Phony Diamond Dust

After Kitty's happy birthday dinner on Friday night Tom helped Diane clear the dining table. The warm effects of prosecco lingered while she gathered the flatware for washing.

"Kitty truly enjoyed this," Diane said, pleased.

Tom had undone his shirttails from his best jeans' waistband. "Kitty's a gracious woman and appreciative. It's easy to do nice things for her. With her husband gone, she needs some attention."

Diane fell silent for a minute. "Especially on her birthday. So I couldn't spoil the evening for her with what I've found out."

Tom glanced at her. "How's that?"

"Yesterday, Chelsea's best friend Jennifer told me that Mermaid Nerissa was planning to leave her job and get into marine research. Kitty will be stunned to hear this, and I don't have all the answers yet."

Tom nudged her arm with his elbow. "Then let the sleeping dog lie until you're ready."

"For now, I should." She thought back. "And while Jennifer talked, I got the strong hunch Chelsea hadn't given her the whole story either about changing jobs and why."

Tom picked up the creamed spinach serving dish with his healthy hand. "There had to be a helluva reason for her to leave Apollo, write off that kind of money, give up the fandom, and throw away years of training."

"Exactly," Diane underscored emphatically. "I suspect it was for more than super frustration over Apollo wanting her to do an additional show. She had also said she wanted to do something more meaningful with her life."

"That's rather philosophical, introspective."

"Mature." She blew out the dinner tapers. "She never got to keep her meeting with Apollo. He expected it was about her probably wanting time off so she and Luke could run off and get married."

Tom set the dish down on an empty platter. "He didn't know he was dealing with a tempest in a teapot."

She picked up plates and paused. "And it was a different kind of tempest." Hands full, she turned and reentered the kitchen with Tom. He carried placemats draped over his bandaged hand and wine glasses in the other.

"Human behavior usually follows needs and emotions. We do what we do in order to exist and survive and all that, you know. And there were some reports that Chelsea seemed afraid of something. This points to the lack of a basic of human need."

"And that is?" Tom asked, depositing the mats and glasses on the counter.

"To feel and be safe." She freed her hands of the plates at the sink. "And if Chelsea was afraid, she wasn't feeling safe."

"From a heavy-duty, serious threat would be my guess."

"Nothing had turned up in her mail, e-mails, or texts according to Detective Brooks. Maybe she was just caving from the pressure."

"Oh, I don't know," Tom said with doubt. "She was used to pressure."

"She hadn't even told Luke of her wish to leave Blue Wave for a marine research job."

"Hmm. That is a stretch."

Diane walked with him back into the dining room and stopped at the buffet. "Kitty loved the ice sculpture and the cake…and our company. She's a bit lonely."

Tom grunted his agreement. "You can count this evening as a success, Hostess Phipps."

Diane smiled. He had a way with words at the most important of times.

Tom came to her side and nodded at the sculpture. "Chef Eric does good work. Did you notice the details in the wing feathers? The etching on its neck? This whole thing sparkles."

"He uses a substance he calls 'diamond dust.' There's a big jar of it in his ice room."

Tom looked amused. "Phony diamond dust. It's a lot less expensive, but works."

"It's really ground iridescent mother of pearl. Ingenious isn't it?"

Tom signaled thumbs up with his good one. His other thumb hadn't seen the light of day since his last check-up at Mayo three days earlier.

"It's too bad this special sculpture won't last the night," she added wistfully. Sometimes beautiful things were so fleeting. Like falling stars, rare ghost orchids, and disappearing mermaids.

~ * ~

The next morning, Diane awakened late. She rolled over and found Tom gone from his side of their bed. Groggy, she sat up and craved coffee. Ten minutes later, she put a pod into the coffee maker and walked out onto the patio. Tom was talking with someone on his cell phone.

"Look, I don't know if I'm the right guy for that one. I don't have blond hair, I'm not forty years old yet, and I don't live in Phoenix."

Diane slowed by a hawthorn bush. Dread tumbled through her while his conversation went on. It meant Tom would leave soon. One would think she'd be used to that by now. She silently prayed this assignment wouldn't be as long as the last. Or as dangerous.

He hung up and looked over at her. "In three days, I'll get a clean bill of health from the doctor, and then I'm going to Phoenix. Counterfeiters."

Diane nodded. "Oh." She dipped back into the kitchen and came out with coffee for them both. "Isn't there enough surveillance work in Florida?"

Tom chuckled. "It's only for two weeks. A special government request."

She gazed at her husband's wounded hand. "Why you?"

"There's rock climbing involved, and I learned how to rappel in the Corps."

She curled the corner of her mouth into a playful smile. "And you'll call me every day."

Tom looked at her reproachfully. "I do my best. There's also a bonus involved."

She sat next to him. "Is that like hazardous duty pay?"

He scoffed, "Hell, I earn that every week."

Diane set her coffee down on a rock planter and took his wounded hand in hers. "So, how're you going to rappel with this?"

Tom grinned mischievously. "I'm not. I'll be visiting a certain outdoor outfitter, the infamous Lena Squashblossom, to buy climbing shoes, ropes, and—"

"Wait. Lena Squashblossom?" She crinkled her nose.

"Right," he said without a blink. "Then I'll stand in an apartment with a partner. We'll be keeping company with a high definition camera aimed at her shop a block away. Eight hours on, eight off. A third and fourth guy will make trips up into the hills to 'drop in' on her operation in a cave. But by then, I should be on my way back home."

Diane twirled the ribbon on her pajama top. "In that case, I'll help you pack."

Tom squeezed her knee with his hand and tossed a nod toward the open patio door. "Your cell phone's ringing."

Tempted not to answer it, Diane stalled until habit pushed her to her feet. She made it inside to the counter on the last ring. "Diane here. Hello, Detective Brooks. Did the Jumbo Shrimp win?"

"Eight to six." he said flatly.

"Well, that's good news."

He skipped a beat. "Here's better good news."

"There's a fingerprint match from the photos?"

Now he sighed. "That's in progress, Ms. Phipps. Patience, please. We've apprehended the con-artist impersonator. Bight Kepler will no longer interfere with our work or con people."

Diane rested her hand on the counter and exhaled in relief. "Congratulations." While she listened, her gaze traveled through the arch to the dining room where the ice sculpture catch pan still rested on the buffet. "May I ask where you found him?"

"At The Poles on the beach. He was with Hannah Hart."

Diane had never been punched in the midriff, but the shock of this news had the same effect. "*What?* She couldn't stand him."

"Sounds about right. They got into it. He slugged her and somebody called nine-one-one. A witness reported they argued about money and a wad of it hit the air. Hannah's at Beaches Baptist Hospital with a mild concussion. Hold it, I've got another call. Oh it's the mayor. Bye."

"Bye," Diane said to dead air. She scrambled to make sense of why Hannah and the infamous Louis had linked up at the beach

Muddled, she moved to the dining room. There were still things to do and she got to it.

Open the hurricane blinds. "Done," she muttered to herself. Straighten the chairs around the table. "Done." Empty the water-filled deep tray that had held the ice sculpture. "In progress," she said, mimicking Brooks' tone. Lifting it in her arms, she took it to the kitchen sink.

Twilight from the window played over the mother of pearl. It shimmered like opalescent sea salt. She couldn't bear to throw it away. How beautiful it would be sprinkled over the pebbles of the potted silk orchid at her office. Silk, because she didn't have a green thumb.

With repurposing in mind, Diane lined a sizable strainer with a smooth, white tea towel. Carefully, she tilted the pan to use a corner as a spout and poured Eric's sculpture water through the thin cotton to catch the pretty sediment. After setting the tray aside, she removed the towel from the strainer and laid it to dry on the granite island surface. Later she could brush the grains coating it into a cup for instant use. *Little things,* she thought brightly. Oh, how little tiny things had the power to make a difference in big ways. Like what she'd spotted in Kitty's photos…

Nineteen

New Evidence

By early afternoon, Tom left to meet Edward, a widowed aeronautics instructor who had invited him for a cool one at the golf club.

"Grilled shrimp for dinner," Diane called after him on his way out. Satisfaction spread through her. Tom had given up good happy hour buddies when they'd moved here. The nineteenth hole offered a place for him to meet and bend elbows with some new peeps.

This also gave Diane another stretch of uninterrupted time at her office. She changed into cotton crop pants and a rosy-peach sleeveless shirt with dainty white daisy buttons. A new pair of cork-bottomed sandals and the gold hoop earrings Tom had given her finished off her Saturday office attire. She returned to the kitchen and put the dry sifted mother of pearl granules in a plastic bag, which she tucked into her oversized tote filled with files, notes, and photos.

In less than thirty minutes, Diane unpacked the things in her office. She sprinkled Eric's diamond dust on the pebbles around the orchid plant resting on the windowsill behind her desk.

"Perfect," she sang in C and turned on the computer.

She answered most of the emails that had piled up, walked into the case board room, and reconstructed the collection of elements pertinent to the case. Hannah Hart's promo postcard and Louis Dresden's business card stuck out to her like sore thumbs. *Why did these two most incompatible people meet at a beach?* circled in her mind like a brown pelican ready to plunge into the sea for a meal.

Diane soon took a short break. She stepped outside for a moment, too, into the gentle air. A chainsaw buzzed close by. Undoubtedly, a trimmer worked on cleaning up palm trees. He pared away shaggy dead fronds, giving the trees a fresh makeover.

Diane decided she should do the same for the case. She needed to cut away the chaff and expose the heart of the Mermaid Nerissa case. Her questions piled up fast. Did the mermaid die because of threatened power? Could be. Did the mermaid die because of jealousy? Perhaps. Did she die because of money? Hardly. So then, did the mermaid die because of politics? Hmm.

Or, did Nerissa die because of something she knew that she shouldn't have? No indication of that. Did the mermaid die because of secret sex? Unlikely, Diane figured. If those questions about motive weren't enough, WHO did it, what was the murder weapon, and what happened to it?

Fighting discouragement, Diane went back inside. She'd devoted herself to making a difference in people's lives by ridding society of low-life trouble. But maybe she wasn't cut out for this line of work after all. The errant thought was too painful to entertain. If Tom knew, he would calmly say, "Nobody ever said this was easy. Get back to work, dear, and we'll celebrate when you've solved the case. And I know you will."

Back at work, Diane read an action reminder to herself. *Check out bio mineral calcium carbonate/crystalline aragonite.* Indeed. This was the curious, almost undetected substance found in Chelsea's wound.

Settling into her desk chair, she pulled the computer keyboard closer, searched the substance, and waited. Reading the description, Diane widened her eyes. She re-read, making sure she hadn't made a mistake. *Iridescent nacre.* More reading clarified: The substance was *mother of pearl.*

Diane's mouth fell open. *Eric's diamond dust?* She sat motionless. Jumping to conclusions would only buy her trouble if she didn't take the next step. She shoved herself to her feet, rounded her desk, and grabbed the orchid from the sill. Carefully, she brushed the iridescent granules back into the plastic bag.

A half hour passed and Diane once again burst into Beau Brooks' cubicle.

"You're back so soon, Ms. Phipps?" Frankly, he didn't sound much better after his mandatory baseball game break. But his eyes twinkled.

She waved the bag at him. "Not soon enough for my taste. But if this checks out, we'll have a break in the Mermaid Nerissa case." She backtracked and shared what she'd learned about infusing ice sculptures with reflective materials for effect. She included how she had Eric's mother of pearl in her possession. All of which justified her interruption to what looked like another busy time for him, despite that it was Saturday afternoon.

"We need a positive match between this and what was found in Chelsea Graham's wound. The M.E. had made a note she'd kept a smear of it in-house." Her case made, she folded her hands together in her lap and waited for comment.

Detective Brooks leaned toward her. "I don't say this very often, lady...but you rock." He took the bag from her hand. "We'll handle it from here. And before you ask, we still don't have a fingerprint ID from the torn up picture of Chelsea."

In less than two days, she'd brought him two key elements. A sense of pride rose in her she hadn't felt in a while. One step at a time to solve a crime.

"Okay." She stood and turned to leave.

He stopped her with, "I'm wondering if you might pay Ms. Hannah Hart a courtesy visit? See what she has to say about Louis Dresden. He only repeats his three aliases over and over."

Diane stilled. "Sure, I'll go see Hannah and report back."

He raised a forefinger. "Better yet, why not wear a wire?"

"I haven't ever worn one, but if you think it'll help, count me in."

"Good. See Sergeant O'Brien in the supply room for that, and thanks."

"Sure."

"Now watch it. Ms. Hart's quirky, temperamental. She threw a stress ball at her wardrobe mistress during my first on-site interview with her."

"I'd noticed your report about that in the files." Diane agreed with his accurate assessment. But what could he expect from a fairly rebellious, free-spirited, and pressured mermaid who craved the attention of a brilliant star?

"I'll add the visit to my schedule."

He issued her a wry half-smile. "Promise?"

Diane turned on her heel. "You really need to go to more ballgames," she uttered and took off unscathed.

"That base is covered, it seems," Detective Brooks called after her.

Twenty

Visiting Hours

After spending Sunday with Tom and devoting a mega-watt thought session to Chelsea's case at her office, Diane followed through on her promise on Monday. She dressed semi-professionally for the occasion and arrived at the hospital mid-morning during visiting hours. Hannah Hart laid half covered with a sheet and slept on her side when Diane entered her room.

Diane gazed at her from the end of the bed, and then settled in the chair next to her. She welcomed the chance to study the patient at will. Hannah breathed steadily. Her hair curled over her cheek and a purple bruise marred the side of her puffed mouth. Her fingers clutched the edge of the sheet. Her nails were broken and an abrasion marred her knuckles.

Diane gazed out the window for a moment. It was a hard adjustment to make from seeing Hannah healthy and made up for work to seeing her crumpled and damaged like this. But considering why Louis Dresden had paid visits to key people associated with victims, Diane harbored a strong hunch why Hannah ended up this way. He'd honed in on an incriminating secret Hannah was keeping and made sure they'd met.

When Diane refocused on Hannah, she was looking at Diane with one eye open.

"Ah, you're awake," Diane said softly.

Hannah lowered her eyelid. "I don't want to talk to anybody. So just leave, please."

Diane pulled her chair closer and waited for Hannah to turn over on her back.

"How're you feeling?"

She stared at the ceiling with indifference. "Like a million dollars, thanks."

Hannah's right eye was black and swollen. Stitches met her eyebrow. Her ear was bandaged and her speech slow. The hospital gown had slipped from her shoulder and Diane pushed it back up in place. She returned the light sarcasm with, "I imagine so," and pulled her little notebook from her purse for effect.

Hannah sputtered, "Nobody can *imagine* how I am, how I feel, how I got this way…and how soon am I getting out of here?"

Diane kept her tone gentle and chatty. "When you're ready, I suppose."

Hannah brushed away a tear. "I'm missing work."

"I'm sure your fans are missing you."

"Well, I'm sure my junior stand-in is doing her best."

"Would you like a drink of water?"

Hannah nodded slightly. "I'll need a straw."

Diane set aside her notebook and busied herself with pouring water and stripping the paper from the straw she plucked from a tall cup. "I'm sorry…there's no lemon here."

Hannah shrugged and held the water glass with both hands. After a few sips from the straw, she handed the glass back to Diane, who rolled the bed table further up to Hannah's waist and set the glass in arm's reach. Diane noticed two white pills in a small white paper cup.

"Are you supposed to take these?"

"I'm not going to. I'll beat this on my own." Hannah pointed at her maimed face.

"They'll probably make you feel better," Diane coaxed. She sat down again and moved her notebook to her lap.

Hannah scowled. "What makes me feel better is that they took him away. He *hit* me." Tears burst forth. "I was doing what he'd asked the best I could, but he hit me. Twice."

Diane moistened her lips. "I'm a little confused," she said softly. "Could we start at the beginning? Who're you talking about?"

"That mangy, jackass private detective I told you about when you came to see me about Nerissa. He came back another time. I tried to get rid of him, and he wouldn't go."

Diane shook her head. "What did he want?" She had a hunch, but carried through.

More tears let loose. "Something I couldn't give him all at once, and he knew that when we met at the beach. But he hit me anyway."

Diane wrote in her notebook. "So it was money he wanted?"

"Ten thousand dollars, Ms. Phipps. And, no, I didn't owe it to him. It was hush money. He'd found out that I had gotten into a big argument with Nerissa about our salaries. He said with what had happened to Nerissa, any difficulty I might've had with her wouldn't look good. I could end up in jail from it. And the last thing I wanted was for the law to come breathing down my neck. He told me he was going to Apollo with what he knew."

"You were upset with your pay?"

"It all started because one day I'd opened the wrong paycheck and saw what Nerissa had earned for one week's work." She paused. "I'm sorry, but it just turned me pea green for a moment. I almost tore up her check, but she came in and found me with it. That's when she blew up, and I blew up back, and then we both were called into Apollo's office. He encouraged us to settle our differences. I had apologized, but Louis reminded me of something else that had happened when I got mad another time, and—"

Diane held up her hand. "So Louis Dresden was blackmailing you?"

Hannah tapped the edge of the bed table with her shaky fingers. "For ten thousand of my savings dollars. You can see why I didn't say anything to you or Detective Book, Baker, Buck-Naked, or something like that."

"Brooks," Diane offered.

Hannah turned her face toward Diane. "Could you raise my bed? My back hurts."

Diane obliged her and resettled. "So, you met Louis on the beach and you gave him the money. Then he became angry?"

Hannah emitted a harsh laugh. "That's right. He blew up partly because it wasn't in one hundred dollar bills. Can you believe that? Again, I'm glad this is over." She raised her fingertips to her puffy eye. "This looks pretty bad, doesn't it? I haven't seen a mirror since I came in here. I guess they want it that way, huh? Anyway, I still owed Louis another five thousand. We were to meet again in a month."

She took Hannah's hand. "If it's any consolation, you were not alone. He's done this kind of thing to other people who were connected in one way or another to homicide victims. The other people had stories to tell that could have thrown suspicion their way. Nobody likes that kind of trouble, and he preyed on that. Now, you rest up, and I'll catch your show at Blue Wave soon."

Diane could've pushed this further, but instinct told her to stop.

Hannah's soulful eyes filled with comfort. "You know, you're really good at your job, Ms. Phipps. Would you stay and have lunch with me? The food here isn't bad, and maybe there's time yet to order another tray." She tapped the call button and a light went on over her bed.

Diane glanced at her purse. Spending more time here wasn't a problem for her, and the covert audio surveillance wire could work for hours.

"Sure, I'll stay for lunch." She was glad for more time with Hannah. This was the most straight up she'd ever seen her. Maybe it really was true that Diane had a gift for people opening up and spilling their guts, worries, woes, successes, and souls, whether she knew them or not.

Either way, there were still a few untouched items Diane wished to explore with Hannah. Feeling warm, she removed her loose pink overshirt and readied for what was to come, including a hospital lunch.

"I wish they'd come," Hannah soon said in a huff. "I'm hungry *now*, and I'm ready for my walk." Opening a magazine, she flipped through the pages faster and faster. "I swear if I had Louis Dresden in front of me right now, I'd squash him like a bug." She hit the top of the table with her fist. "I feel so stupid."

Diane couldn't blame her. Her cell phone rang and she checked the screen. Detective Brooks requested a call-back. "Hannah, excuse me for a moment. I need to step out into the hallway."

The injured mermaid turned her gaze out the window. "Take your time. I'm sure not going anywhere. Except down for two trips to the nurses' station and back after lunch. Big whoop."

Diane exited the room and walked at a good clip toward the women's room. It was empty inside and quiet. She made the call. "Yes, Detective Brooks?"

He dispensed with his usual greeting. "Good. You're staying for lunch with Hannah."

She confirmed, although it wasn't necessary. He was somewhere off-site catching every word of her conversation with Hannah.

"Over your ice cream, maybe you can get her to explain why she tore up Chelsea Graham's photos. We have one-hundred percent thumbprint match for Hannah on the photo you brought in here."

Surprised, Diane asked, "Hannah's prints are on record?"

"She worked at a kids' summer camp four years ago, which required her prints. So, listen up. You take a five-by-seven glossy picture facing front and tear it into fourths. Your thumbprint ends up in two places on the first tear and two on the next. Got it?"

Diane held her phone tighter to her ear. "Yes, except tearing up pictures isn't a crime."

"Usually not. Hannah obviously lost it over an issue she had with Chelsea. You're on a roll there with her. She's loosening up. Maybe you can pull more truth out of this lovely mermaid? Find out what happened? Beyond arresting the sleaze-bag con-artist, I still have an unsolved murder on my watch. And right now *every spat and everyone* is suspect. Later."

As he hung up Diane looked at herself in the mirror over the sink. *Truth*. It was such a short, impactful word. Could she siphon more truth out of Hannah? Where would it lead? To a killer's doorstep? Furthermore, if Eric's diamond dust matched the substance in Chelsea's wound, Diane harbored a new, rip-roaring theory how it got there.

She shook her head. Despite her work for her client Kitty on this mermaid case, there were so many balls still in the air. Raising her chin with determination, she was going to catch every single one of them.

As she re-entered Hannah's room, a familiar ding rang loud and clear over the P.A. system. "Patient visiting hours are now over," the voice said. "Have a nice day. Thank you."

Quickly, Diane forgot lunch and promised Hannah she'd come see her again the next day.

"Come earlier, okay?" Hannah asked.

"For sure," Diane said and patted her hand. "Now, you rest up."

With that, she left the room and called Brooks.

"I heard," he said, cutting her off. "I want to hear more about Dresden."

Diane nodded. "And I want to know about those torn-up pictures."

"My money's still on Eric Jameson," he said bluntly.

She rolled her eyes. "I'm seeing her again tomorrow. I've gotta go now. There's still time before the matinee performance at Blue Wave for me to check out something."

"What?" Brooks barked.

Diane sighed. "Back to you later."

Twenty-one

From All Angles

Diane walked into Blue Wave and headed for the Deck Café. She was famished. The place was almost full of guests having lunch. Colored umbrellas shaded the chairs and tables. Oversized menus brimmed with seafood choices. Living in Florida was agreeing with her.

"I'll have the chilled shrimp, please," she told the waiter. "With unsweetened iced tea."

Her stomach was growling, but she'd make this quick. On her way there, she'd passed Neptune's Grotto and given the driftwood door handle a tug. The door opened easily. She peeked inside. The room was quiet and dim. No movement except for a cleaning lady wiping down the glass front to the show aquarium. Diane was hoping for nobody.

The sign on the tripod outside the door said, "Matinee Performance at 3:00 p.m."

So she had just enough time to grab some food and get back to the Grotto by two o'clock. If she had company then, she'd still come up with a way to do what she needed to do.

Thankfully, the food service on the Deck was fast. She ate quickly and watched the water. No two days at the beach were alike. The breeze and light on the ocean were ever-changing, same with the clouds. Today, though, the sky was clear. Only a parasailer dotted the field of blue, and the silhouette of a ship on the horizon and pelicans alighting on the water gave her entertainment while she dipped shrimp into cocktail sauce.

Finished, Diane wiped her fingers with a wet, lemon-scented cloth. She paid the bill and made her way back to Neptune's Grotto. Reentering the room kind of gave her a chill. Air conditioning at the resort ran strong. This was Florida, after all. Two other things had been niggling her since she had awakened. The first was over something Tom had recently reminded her about: Look at things from all angles. The second one was the crime scene photo of Chelsea's bloodied finger stripe on the show tank glass. Thus, she had made tracks back.

Also, Diane's mind kept asking, "What if?"

It was the mother of all questions that kept her awake nights. As usual, it begged for an answer from her.

"So, *what if* Chelsea knew her attacker?" she whispered to herself as she stepped into the room. The query came out of left field, even though it was a strong possibility often considered during homicide investigations. Yet, nothing had come from Detective Brooks about it. But still, this was, by far, the most intriguing question of late.

Luck was with Diane. She was alone. Wending her way through the tables, she arrived at the front of the room. Just she and the show tank were meeting up again. She pulled from her bag the photocopy of the official crime scene photo No. 37, which she'd requested from Forensics.

She held it up in front of her, getting a good foothold on where the photographer had stood to take it. She was apparently shorter than the photographer, so her perspective was slightly off. But that was the point. She yearned to check the streaked finger stripe from different angles. She suspected doing so might tell a new story.

She stood directly in front of where the bloody comet was left on the glass. It was positioned low, very close to the floor, and drawn by Chelsea inevitably in her last seconds. Diane bent at the waist so her face was closer to where the stripe would've been on the glass. Then, she got down on her knees.

Viewing the evidence from this angle changed things. The slant looked different, and the imprint seemed to change in size. The starting point seemed thicker from down there. The ending point weakened as it trailed down the surface.

Had Chelsea deliberately poked her finger hard at the top and against the surface and let it trail off on purpose? It was a long shot, but it seemed so. Why so hard? So deliberate? Was she trying to tell us something? Her hunch was, yes.

Diane's curiosity rivaled her decorum. She went the extra mile, lowering herself the whole way to the carpet. Arranging herself in the position she'd seen in the photographs of Chelsea's dead body, she pretended to be her. She pulled her lipstick from her pocket and drew upon the glass as closely as she could to where Chelsea had left her mark. With her eyes, she followed the direction from bottom to top, instead of vice versa.

Every fiber of Diane's being told her she was looking at a directional arrow. She searched for where it ended, letting her gaze take in the seascape features close to it. From down here, it was pointing directly to the top of the large, rounded brain coral on the right side of the underwater landscaping.

She blinked and sat upright. All of her little I'm-on-to-something-here nerves prickled.

"Why point there?" she blurted.

Suddenly, the house lights blasted awake, almost blinding her. She jerked herself back up to her knees and peered over the top of the closest table. Apollo Redstone walked toward the front. He stopped in his tracks upon seeing her.

"Hello, Ms. Phipps," he said amicably. "What're you doing in here by yourself?"

Diane's cheeks heated up. "Oh, hi. I was revisiting the crime scene." She scrubbed the red line off the glass with her shirttail and stashed the lipstick back into her pocket. Rising to her feet, she said, "Didn't want to bother anyone."

Apollo smiled. "How's it going with your investigation?"

Diane picked up her purse and stuffed the photocopy inside. "Actually, okay. Thanks. I visited Hannah Hart today. She's in good hands now."

"I sent flowers. Her stand-in Lexie is working well enough, for now. But we're all eager for our Hannah to be in the aquarium again."

"She'll be happy to hear that, I'm sure." She looked at her watch. "Oh my, it's almost two-forty five. Showtime is at three, right?"

He pushed his hands into his pockets. "It is. You should stay to watch it with me."

Diane felt cornered, but it was a good idea. "Okay. That'd be nice, thank you."

They crossed to a stage left table, and she sat in the chair Apollo pulled out for her. Staff filed into the room from the front doors and the room sprang to life. Music played from speakers overhead, while patrons arrived and took seats. Waiters brought drinks and silver bowls of snacks to each table. Candles in amber glass holders shed a glow onto people's faces.

Diane had no trouble figuring out why this show venue took top prizes in the hotel industry. The special lighting in the tank slowly came up full tilt. Diane relaxed a bit and enjoyed the whimsical production. She shook her head sometimes in disbelief at how the talented cast expertly made their moves. From their side of the glass, each swimmer connected with the audience, adding intimacy.

Apollo remained in affable spirits through the show and shared bits of information throughout. Forty minutes later, Diane and he applauded heartily with everyone else.

One by one, the principals and the support cast each drifted into their final places for an underwater version of a curtain call. Diane remembered the photograph of the same setup from when Chelsea held the role of Head Mermaid Nerissa. It was like déjà vu.

Perched on the broad front lip of the giant clamshell sat Hannah's stand-in for Mermaid Nerissa. Holding a scepter, Lexie waved it slowly through the water. Green sparkles floated from the head. The creamy, fluted clamshell lid behind her twinkled with tiny silver lights, giving this temporary Nerissa an aura. The audience erupted again into applause.

The newer Merman Triton, looking royal and handsome, drifted close to her side and held her free hand. Whistles rose from around the room for him. When Hannah had assumed Chelsea's role as Mermaid Nerissa, Lexie had been found to take Hannah's role of Mermaid Salacia. For now, she'd been bumped up to play Nerissa, until Hannah returned.

Lexie smiled and sat on top of the rounded pink brain coral, swishing her tail. The other two support cast members adorned other features of the landscape and bowed their heads. Drifting into the shadows, they each soon exited through the rocky grotto at the rear of the seascape.

Mermaid Nerissa remained in a spotlight for a solo farewell. Her hair floated and her magnificent tail draped down to the sand in front of her. She taunted the guests with a flirting tail tip wave. Then the music swelled, and after she blew a final kiss, all went dark.

Undoubtedly, the opulent scene soon would be lost in the mish mash of fun experiences for guests at Blue Wave.

But the magical ending had burned itself into Diane's memory. Seeing the live show was much better than looking at the post card she had back her office. The cast arrangement looked the same as when Chelsea held the role of Mermaid Nerissa. So, Diane gave Apollo quick credit. He had the good sense not to fix what wasn't broken.

Hours later, tucked in bed with her case notes spread over her lap, Diane bolted upright.

She snatched up the show photo and showed Tom.

"What's that about?" he asked, closing a book.

"It's my case solved, is what it is. Now, all I need is proof."

He winked at her. "And a weapon?"

"We'll never have the weapon," she declared. "Never. It's gone…trust me."

"Always."

Twenty-two

Oh, My

Diane decided early the next morning that she'd keep her lunch date with Hannah. She also arrived early. A small coffee pot sat on Hannah's bed table, which Diane helped herself to in a Styrofoam cup, and a cookie laying on an almost bare plate. The visit began pleasantly with Hannah sharing a few childhood and college stories. She soon lapsed into her first performance with Chelsea.

"I was fresh off the plane from Miami when I came to Blue Wave to work. It was so fun for me to join the troupe. Nerissa met me in the lobby and showed me the ropes early on. I felt lucky to work with her because she was advanced in her techniques. She wasn't selfish about sharing things, and we'd even swum in the outside pool after hours for more practice."

"You must miss her," Diane said, finishing up a cookie.

"Sometimes I do, yes."

She brushed a crumb from the corner of her mouth. "You grew apart?"

"Well, I think of it more as we grew more professional. There were times when I thought she was too much of a perfectionist, to be honest. If I swished my tail two times to the right instead of three times after a back flip, I'd hear about it. She and Sam were alike that way. They were sticklers for detail. I could get frustrated with them, but someday I'd also be a master mermaid and could then do things my way more often."

Diane laid one hand over the other in her lap. "That must've helped."

Hannah nodded. "Most people don't really get what we do. Under the water, we become larger than life. We transform ourselves into fantasy characters, and adding flourishes comes naturally to me. We're also athletes. I still work hard on fitness and extending my breath holds." She pushed her coffee cup. "But Nerissa was truly the queen. When she'd put on her tail and slip into the tank, I'd swear the water got warmer."

Diane thought aloud. "For sure, the lights got brighter, and the publicity got stronger."

Hannah cast a rueful glance. "Like I'd said, Nerissa had *everything*. Even now, I'll never reach her level of talent. Sam knows it, and so do I," charged from her swollen lips. "But I'm the top-billing mermaid now. What Nerissa did is pretty much history. Things really do change. Techniques change. Apollo's happy, and that's all that matters to me."

Diane pulled herself forward in the chair. "Good on you. You've persevered and you won." She pulled her purse to her lap and opened it. "I have a few postcards of you and the show I bought from the gift shop. Would you mind autographing one for me?"

Hannah took it in her hand. "Pen, please?"

"Oh, of course." Diane dug deeper and retrieved one without dislodging the tiny wire transmitter parked next to her lipstick. "I think that is a wonderful promo picture of you, by the way. I guess you and Nerissa often posed for pictures?"

A shadow passed through Hannah's eyes. "Every other Friday we had a publicity call. Prints were made from our pictures for posters and postcards. Neptune's Grotto has its own website to update. There's always a big marketing effort to keep things current." She signed the photograph with her right hand, and Diane reclaimed it.

Hannah's gaze fell to the blanket. Her voice lowered. "Ms. Phipps, have you ever made a mistake you've truly regretted from almost the minute you made it?"

Diane stepped up to the virtual plate. "I have, yes. Most of us do."

A sigh came from the patient. "Well, I like talking with you, and I've never told anyone this. Not long before Nerissa was found dead, we had gone through one of our routine Friday promo calls. The next week, we each got a set of courtesy prints from that session for our own use. Nerissa had become so testy with me...with all of us, really." She brushed away lint fuzz from the white blanket. "As you know, I don't handle nitpicking or being micro-managed very well."

"Yes, I can see that. You're a person who strives for the big picture." She tapped Hannah's photo for emphasis. "It's just your way."

The mermaid quieted. "I'm not proud of it, but the last batch of photos arrived while I was alone in our dressing room. My mood wasn't the best because, for the third time that week, Nerissa had commented on my messy vanity and how I liked to listen to the Beach Zombies on the radio while I put on make-up." She frowned. "It was really getting old for me. She needed a taste of her own nastiness. So, I opened her photo envelope, and I tore up all her perfect little pictures and put them back inside."

Diane feigned a jaw drop. "No gold stars for that one, but...you probably felt better."

Hannah smiled peevishly. "I did for a short time, and then I left for the day."

Diane's thoughts raced over how Hannah had acted out her contempt for Chelsea. Was it merely the tip of a grudging, envious iceberg? Her intuition rumbled, and there was only one way to know for sure.

She girded herself for an indignant outburst, tilted her head, and lightly suggested, "This act was probably not as good as you felt when you took Nerissa's life? Then, 'Poof!' she was gone, and you walked out into the spotlight forever."

Hannah jerked upright. "Excuse me? What're you saying?"

Diane cleared her throat. "I think, Hannah, that the time has come for you to share with me about what happened the night Mermaid Nerissa died." She put it out there simply, with no emotion dripping from her words. She didn't raise her eyebrows, or use a judgmental tone. But in case of a Hannah melt-down, Detective Brooks was on audio standby.

Hannah shuddered and leveled an icy glare on Diane. "Are you thinking or *imagining*?" She pushed her hands against the side of the portable table and shoved it forward with all her might. Smacking against the footboard, it swiveled around, scattering all things on top to the floor, bed, and at Diane. The vase filled with flowers from Apollo narrowly missed her chest and crashed to the tiles, spewing glass and blossoms everywhere.

"I more than think. I know, Hannah. *I know*."

Diane left no room for doubt in her voice. It was a risky ploy, she knew. Hannah would either clam up or succumb to giving up. It had to be a lot of effort keeping a murder locked up inside one's conscience…if there was one still working. She bet Hannah's was. Guilt had led her to share her story about the torn-up photos. Guilt and human conscience went hand-in-hand.

The air tightened around her and Hannah like a noose. Despair contorted the mermaid's already injured face. Pulling up her knees, she buried her head in her palms. "You have no idea what it was like...to report every day for another dose of being around Nerissa and her wretched *greatness*."

Diane rose from the chair and laid her hands palms down on the edge of the bed. "Maybe I do, and maybe I don't, but all of that didn't bring out the best in you, did it?"

Hannah slowly lifted her head. "It was getting worse at the end, because something was eating at her, and she took it out on me and others. She didn't let up, even though it was the Summer Splash Bash. Besides, she was suffocating me with all her twitter, and expensive, fancy tails, and her super fans."

Using her most subdued style of active listening, Diane prompted, "So you put together a plan, and—"

"Ha," Hannah exclaimed. "No plan was needed. After the last show and how she delayed those two cues, which could've made *me* look bad, I invited her for a chat in Neptune's Grotto." She gazed ceilingward and went back in her memory. "It was very dim in there, and she had no idea I'd come in from the back and hid behind the pillar near the tank."

Diane kept her cool. "Go on, Hannah. You've come this far."

More tears came, and Hannah asked for her bag. "I really need to hold my grandmother's handkerchief for more of this." She pointed to the locker, and Diane reluctantly brought the bag to her.

"Thank you." Hannah set it in her lap and pulled out a cloth hankie with printed violets and pressed it against her wet cheeks. "My grandmother was a great lady," she said, her chin quivering. "It's good she's not here to see this." She stuffed the hankie back into the bag and sniffled on. "It didn't take long, you know. I came at her from behind and stabbed her right in her curving, damn swan neck. I couldn't put up with her anymore! I slipped through the door to the passageway and went directly to my dressing room. I changed clothes and went to the party out by the pool. My thankless job was done. I'd done us all a favor, see?"

Diane's head spun, and she sank into the chair. "Is there anything else, Hannah? Like maybe you snapped, or you suddenly got a bad headache?"

Hannah pulled her bag closer and peered into it. "Not really, Ms. Phipps. And now you really do *know* it all. And before you go, here's something for you." Swiftly, she pulled a small revolver from the bag and shakily aimed it at Diane.

"You're going to shoot me?" Diane cried loudly and distinctly for the mic to pick up.

"Don't even think about your cell phone. I'm done, and so are you."

As she raised the barrel a tad higher, the door to the room burst open behind Diane.

Instinctively, she dove to the floor and rolled under the bed.

"Drop it, Ms. Hart," Detective Brooks bellowed.

In nanoseconds a shot fired off, and Diane reflexively covered her ears. Her heart lost its next beat as she waited for Beau Brooks to fall to the floor.

Twenty-three

Loose Ends

Diane trekked with Tom along the beach two days later. The Mayo doctor had unexpectedly delayed his release. This was their last chance to get out and about before he flew to Phoenix in the morning.

Inbound waves teased Diane's bare feet, and she kicked at their foam with delight.

"Do you feel better now that the mermaid case is solved?" Tom asked, snapping pictures of skittering terns with his cell phone camera. The breeze ruffled his hair from behind, which added to his rugged handsomeness.

"I not only feel better, I'm ready for my next one."

He grinned and nudged her with his elbow. "Nice job."

Diane sighed. "I'm glad Detective Brooks wasn't hurt."

"I'm thankful you weren't either. Close call, there, Private Investigator Phipps."

She slipped her hand into her shorts' pocket. "Hannah's aim was shaky, and she shot the wall. All heck let loose after that—nurses running and patients screaming. When I crawled out from under the hospital bed, Detective Brooks was reciting Hannah her rights for the murder of Chelsea Graham. He was in the next room, and he couldn't have burst in at a better time." She looked up at a box kite swooping in the sky.

"Want to walk on the pier?" Tom interjected.

"Fine with me." They turned around. "Hannah's still in there under twenty-four-hour watch until she can be released. It's such a sad thing, Tom. Her ego and envy of Chelsea got the better of her. Things weren't coming her way fast enough, so she sped them up. It all made perfect sense to her. Apollo called me and left a thank you message. Neptune's Grotto is closed until further notice."

Tom pocketed his cell phone. "What tipped you off to Hannah Hart being the culprit?"

Diane kept her pace next to him. "Because, dear Tom, after I interviewed all those people and sifted through a ton of notes and computer reports and re-visited the crime scene, I finally looked at some things from a different angle. And I finally asked the right question."

Tom slowed to a halt. "And that question was?"

Diane moved in for a hug. "A simple one, really. It all came down to one thing: Who would gain the most from Mermaid Nerissa being gone? I went through the list of interviewees and concluded that no one would as much as Hannah Hart. She got what she wanted. To be Number One Mermaid."

Tom chuckled darkly. "She's Number One Mermaid, out of a job, and will be serving time."

Diane shook her head. "You know, this business is so not pretty."

"I know, my dear," he said and hugged her.

Diane reflected for a minute. "Good part is that dear Kitty can now work on putting the tragedy behind her. She cried last night when Detective Brooks and I visited her to tell her the case is solved.

She was flabbergasted over who'd done it. Apollo also reported that Chef Eric was beside himself when he'd heard about the murder weapon."

Tom stepped back. "About that. How'd you know what it was?"

"Two of Kitty's pictures of the King Neptune ice sculpture carried a clue…and the possible proof. She'd taken one of the photos right before Chelsea's last show for the Summer Splash Bash. Then, while she'd waited for Chelsea after her last show, she snapped another one of the sculpture. The second one didn't look right to me. When I looked at it closer, I realized that the middle prong of King Neptune's trident wasn't there. That meant it went missing not long after the end of the show. Later, I re-read the ME's report with the wound description and the possible weapon was spherical, thick, possibly with a barb at one end of it."

"Very good observation and deduction."

She nodded her thanks. "What brought me even closer was when I looked up the substance that was left in Chelsea's fatal wound. It was mother of pearl! This was Eric's go-to product for making ice sculptures iridescent, remember? What clinched that was I'd taken Eric's diamond dust left in the tray at our house after the sculpture melted to Detective Brooks for a possible match of the substance found in Chelsea's wound."

"And?"

"It did."

"At that point, my suspicion turned in Eric's direction. But there was still no motivation for murder on his part, and his alibi stuck. After Hannah admitted she stabbed Chelsea in the neck, all that was needed was for the two substances to match. Lab confirmation came through late before my second visit. So, when I went back to have lunch with her, I had a victim, a place and time, opportunity, probable means, and the murderer."

She took in a breath and resumed. "Now, I wish I could say I have the murder weapon. The lack of evidence issue has been worrying me since the beginning. But we won't ever have it. The actual murder weapon ice prong from Neptune's trident had melted."

Tom pursed his lips, then, "So Hannah broke off the spike, and—"

"Neptune's Grotto had emptied out after the show and the lights had dimmed. She'd picked her moment."

"Takes a strong hand to do that."

"It would, I agree. But Hannah squeezed stress balls, and she was more athletically built than Chelsea."

"Hmm. She could've knocked it off with something."

"Either way, the ice prong ended up in Hannah's hand. She did the job, and left the scene via the back passageway door, ditched the prong, and went on with her busy evening as if nothing had happened."

Tom whistled. "And that's it?"

She added, "Well, almost…When I'd found out that the blackmailer was picked up on the beach with Hannah, it signaled he was onto something big between Hannah and Chelsea. Like Hannah ripping up pictures? Like their hot disagreements that weren't so secret. That hunch helped fuel me to hype it up and convince Hannah that I *knew* she'd done it. And it worked. She caved and confessed."

"Yeah, but wasn't she under meds when she confessed? Not admissible in court."

"Good points. On my second visit, Hannah told me she felt better and that she'd not taken her meds again the night before. 'I'm bigger than this,' she'd said. 'I don't need them.'"

After she confessed, I'd asked what she did with the weapon. It got kind of creepy because she laughed and recited a riddle. "What do fish and me have in common? A shiny little sparkle in my tail—old, but not forgotten."

"Huh?"

"I know, I know. That tail thing kept bugging me. So I made one quick last trip to Blue Wave and looked up Rosa DeLaCroix. We went to the mermaid dressing room and Rosa showed me the collection of retired tails. There's a whole bin of them back there. Hannah had gotten bigger, and Rosa had to come up with more. The old tails were saved."

Tom raised an eyebrow. "Hey, is this when I went to the bookstore after your adventure at the hospital?"

"Yes, and I was glad you forgot what time it was and took longer."

He shrugged. "Happens with books."

"Yes. It happens with me all the time at art museums. By the way, a Claude Monet exhibit is coming to the Denver Art Museum this fall."

He looked at her knowingly and took the hint. "I hadn't heard, but Denver is always fun. We can see my Aunt Meredith; more than once she's invited us to visit."

"I'll check the exhibit dates. Anyway, I found six purple tails. I spent an hour shining a flashlight down into them looking for some of Eric's diamond dust. Tail number five came up the winner. There it was. A clump of it mounded at the very bottom, along with the clear plastic rod that Eric had used inside the ice prong as a form. Only Hannah knew where she'd put the weapon. I found what was left of it."

"Thank you, Rosa," Tom sang. "Teamwork works, doesn't it?"

"I'd also asked Detective Brooks what they'd found on the broken security system videos. 'Black screens,' he'd said. 'Useless.' I asked if he minded if I looked at them. He rolled his eyes. 'See Bernie in Evidence.'"

"Turns out the security camera problem in Zone eleven was an intermittent issue. It had flicked on for maybe only twenty or thirty seconds at a time. Then it went on the blink again for hours. It was giving Apollo fits, and he told me he'd had the whole system replaced."

Tom nodded.

"Then, another What if? question hit me."

"It's a bitch, isn't it?" he asked.

"A nice one in the end." She pushed strands of hair away from her eyes. "On a long shot, I sat down in that hot, dingy evidence room and ran through what was left behind after the system was torn out of the ceilings. I'd almost given up, except twice the cameras kicked into working order. Short blips, more like flickers of light. But enough!"

"How were they missed?"

"Tired and overworked men who're interrupted a lot is my guess."

"One glimpse showed the musicians setting up in the corridor for a short run. But the best part was the second time. For a mere twenty seconds, another camera had picked up movement in the shadows in Neptune's Grotto. It caught the hazy profile of Hannah Hart letting Chelsea Graham slump to the floor. Hannah had turned her back to flee just as the recording cut out again. Detective Brooks about had a fit and ran that video section through special services for an undeniable clearer image."

Tom beamed. "So, you were right. Hannah Hart killed Chelsea Graham."

She raised her chin. "I think we have a case that'll stick now."

Tom put his hands on her shoulders. "Congratulations, Diane I'm proud of you. When I get back from Phoenix, we'll celebrate."

Diane grinned. "Sounds special and nice."

"Cruises usually are."

She walked with him from the sand up to the old wooden ramp to the Jacksonville Beach Pier gate. He caught her new frown. "What is it?"

"There's still one mystery about this case. I can't get to the bottom of what was bothering Chelsea so much to make her want to leave her Blue Wave life. It *had* to be more than wanting to save sea turtles."

Tom led her through the gate and paid at the window. He scooped her hand up with his and they headed far out to the end of the pier. "Unfortunately, there's a chance you'll never know."

The possibility poked at her. "Yeah, but it's a loose end. You know how they bother me."

"Some things we get to figure out and tie up, and some we don't. Like, see that horizon out there? Is it a perfect line from this side to that?"

She squinted through her sunglasses. "No, there's a boat."

"Do you know who's on that boat?"

She eyed him skeptically. "How would I know that?"

"Neither do I, and does it matter to us? No. But that's a loose end of sorts to somebody. And the boat will sail away and leave a nice clean horizon line after it. So don't fret."

"You're no help," she groused. "I like uncovering truth and tying up *real* loose ends. Getting *all* the facts."

He gave her a playful wink. "Good. Here's my real loose end. Where's my other brown sock? I need to pack it for Phoenix."

Diane folded her arms and squared her chin. "Tom, I didn't tell Kitty again about Chelsea's plan to leave Blue Wave because I don't believe I still have the full story on it. Disclosure to my clients is my responsibility. I want to fully finalize the case with Kitty, leave no stones unturned, and put her mind to total rest."

"Oh, I get it. I was hoping you could give yourself a break. Tying up loose ends won't always happen. Frustration about them can make you feel inept." He ran his hand down his jaw. "Actually, I've been thinking about Kitty."

His insights settled somewhere between her heart and conscience. "How so?"

Tom hesitated. "I think we should introduce my new golf club buddy Edward to her. They're around the same age. He was in education, and she worked in a library. It could work. Do you think she'd be open for that?"

Diane gave it about ten seconds. "She might. She really might be. She's been by herself now for three years. When I see her next, I'll try to bring it up comfortably." She dropped her arms to her side. "Meanwhile, your other sock is gone. It had a hole, and I threw it out."

Tom smooched her on the cheek. "See how the truth rises? Maybe not today or tomorrow, but it probably will about your mermaid case, too. So hang in."

Twenty-four

New Friend

A month later, Diane arrived at her office after lunch for an appointment in a half hour with a possible new gentleman client. She brought a new pitcher of iced tea from the kitchen and set the tray and glasses on her desk. When the front door opened behind her, she turned and raised her eyebrows in surprise.

"Hello," she greeted the woman who walked timidly into the room. "May I help you? I'm Diane Phipps."

"Yes, Ms. Phipps, I'm glad to meet you. My name is Megan Young. I...I don't have an appointment, but Detective Brooks sent me your way." She held up a slip of paper with directions to Diane's office. "I'd like to talk to you about Chelsea Graham."

Intrigued, Diane invited her in for tea and to sit for a spell in the chintz chair.

"I won't take much time," Megan said. Her sun-streaked hair, held in place on top of her head with sunglasses, fell in layers along her face and covered her bare shoulders. She appeared to be about thirty and wore a halter top and slim pants. Her chocolate brown eyes were tinged with the weight of burden.

Diane sat in her desk chair. "Were you a friend of Chelsea's?"

"A new friend. I'm here to thank you for finding out who murdered her. She was a good person, and we hit it off very well when we first met at the hospital. I was incredibly upset when I learned she'd been killed, and…." Her voice faded.

Diane got up from her desk and pulled an old oak chair across the floor to sit nearer Megan. "I'm sorry you lost your friend, and I'm glad I was able to put the case to rest. So, thank you for coming in to meet with me. This doesn't happen much, except from my clients."

Megan turned to face her. "Chelsea and I shared the same dilemma, and now I've another support group buddy. We're doing well, I'm happy to say."

Diane searched her face. "There are still some questions in my mind about Chelsea. May I ask what dilemma you both shared?"

A frown line deepened on Megan's forehead. "We were both diagnosed with epilepsy on the same day."

Stunned, Diane felt the air leave her lungs.

"Epilepsy?" she stammered.

"Yes, ma'am. We started treatment together and went for counseling at the clinic. This wasn't very long before she passed away, only a matter of weeks. When I went to our next session, they told us Chelsea wouldn't be with us. It was a shock. But before this, we each had written out our personal management plans."

Diane summoned her poise. "That must've been extremely helpful."

"Yes, and what we were facing was difficult to handle at first. Having our conditions meant making big changes in our lives. First, we had to decide whom to tell about it. That part was very hard for us because it brought trouble for people closest to us. Early on, we even went through a short denial about it…hoped it all would go away on its own. Remission can happen, but it's scarce and selective, and who knew if we would be so lucky." She stopped for some tea.

"Do you remember who Chelsea was going to tell about this?"

"She never shared it in group. We each adopted the prescribed medicine regiment. Then, it came to deciding what to do about our jobs. Chelsea faced more risks than me. I taught piano to kids, but she worked mostly underwater in front of a lot of people. Despite treatment and probable odds against it, a seizure could still happen while she was performing. So, Chelsea knew it was the end of her career."

Megan paused. "*That* really messed with her head. Overnight, she grew irritable, testy, even obnoxious with things and people in general. But after a few sessions, we all fell into better alignment with what we needed to do. She calmed down somewhat, same as me."

Spellbound, Diane sat wordless.

"During our last session, Chelsea explained how she had met with the director of a research lab for a new job. She was up front with him and described what was necessary if she got sick while on duty. He told her their whole business was based on conservation and taking care of marine life, so why wouldn't they want to help her if something happened.

"She never got there, though. Instead, an evil woman cut her life short. And I, for one, couldn't be happier to meet people like you, Ms. Phipps, who didn't let her get away with it. Chelsea deserved that much. So, again, thank you." Her voice weakened with emotion as she set her glass on the window sill.

Here it is, Diane thought. *The truth revealed before my eyes.* So, there was a completely understandable reason Chelsea's mood turned stormy and she secretly sought another job. It was a matter of self-preservation. This was what she had wanted to meet Apollo about the day after she died.

Diane barely kept her own emotions in check and gazed at the orchid. Mother of pearl no longer adorned the smooth pebbles around its stem. She touched her temples with her fingers.

"Sorry, I'm rather amazed and am filling in the details where they fit."

Megan nodded patiently. "I'd like to stay longer, but I really must go," she said in the quiet. "We're recording a demo for a country singer at my studio. Once in music, always in music. But it's in a different way now for me."

Diane's admiration rose. "Wait, please. I'm the one who needs to thank you for coming by. Aside from your kind compliment, you've answered my questions, which put my mind to ease. Bless you."

"It's my pleasure and my duty."

Megan and she stood, and Diane escorted her to the door. "Keep in touch, and…I *like* country music."

The woman flashed a smile and walked away.

With only ten minutes to spare before her next appointment arrived, Diane returned to her desk and opened the original file she'd prepared on Chelsea Graham. The last piece of the puzzle had fallen into place. She was happy her intuition hadn't forsaken her. Chelsea did have a deeper motive than saving turtles. She *was* afraid of *something*—not someone.

Diane gazed down at her notes and items she'd tucked inside the folder. Hannah Hart's picture caught her eye, and the bittersweet irony hit her. "If you had waited, Mermaid Salacia, you could've had it *all in less than a month,"* she said aloud and lowered the front flap. "You killed her for nothing."

Now, there was still one thing to do—the royal ritual that Diane indulged in when things were tied up and she could move on. Opening the top right-hand drawer, she pulled out an oversized rubber stamp and red ink pad. She lifted the metal lid and pressed the stamp against the moist spongy surface. Making a quick, resounding move, she pounded the stamp to the folder.

CASE CLOSED.

Satisfied, Diane got up and went into the case board room. She had a spring in her step. Her dream of solving crimes was becoming more real. No longer was what she wanted to do just a dream. She was establishing herself as an intrepid P.I. with a solid future. Tom's admiration had puffed his chest. Even Detective Beau Brooks had sent her an official Certificate of Recognition.

An antique Steelcase cabinet stood in the corner, and she placed the file under G, for Chelsea Graham, Death of a Mermaid. When she returned to her front office, the front door was opening. She walked toward it with her hand outstretched.

"Hello, Mr. Crawford?"

"Indeed, I'm Howard Crawford." His husky frame dwarfed her, and his thick black glasses contrasted his white hair. His smile was faint; his handshake was firm and straightforward.

"I'm Diane Phipps. How can I help you?"

"First, you might get more parking places out front," he said gruffly.

She chortled. "It's a battle, believe me."

"Well, I know all about those," he said ruefully. "But more to the point of my visit, you can help me find out what has happened to my wife's million dollar tiara!"

Diane reclaimed her hand. "Of course, we can work on that together. Come chat with me, have some iced tea, and sit for a spell in my chintz chair."

Meet Karen Hudgins

After Karen Hudgins first tried writing in 1989, she devoted herself to learning the craft and has written nine published works of fiction. She has lived in the East, Midwest, South, and now in Colorado, where her writing continues. Her novels are mostly character-driven, and her degree in behavioral science helps her create credible characters who overcome life's problems, or determinedly find out whodunit. Research, reading, movies, music, photography are fun for her, a life-long learner. She makes use of imagination and promises a happy ending. Karen is a grandmother and also "Mom" to her orange cat. Meeting readers and writers brings her joy.

Other Works From The Pen Of Karen Hudgins

Secrets of the Heart - Molly, boutique owner, secretly believes she's fallen from grace and doesn't deserve goodness like compassionate Julian, master coffee roaster, who also has troublesome secrets—but brews up irresistible true love for her.

When Hearts Speak - Sarah Grace, recently widowed, follows her passion for watercolor painting, which leads her to handsome, enigmatic Wyatt, who slowly reveals his dark torment and love.

Best Man - After a polo accident, a wedding couture designer tangles with her client's best man, a vintner and polo player, who ultimately becomes her best man for life.

Tonight with Tarzan - An interior designer falls for a local "Tarzan," whose work and secret dual identity push her to overcome fears—or lose the love of her life.

Midnight with Maverick - A pastry chef and copper fortune heir find true love despite their backgrounds and the mystery that rocked their families apart twenty years earlier.

One Night with Zorro - A lace proprietor finds the man to fulfill her dreams—except an almost fatal tragedy steers him away from what she also fervently wants—children.

Next Year's Promise - Betrayed in love, a promotions professional vows never to mix business and romantic pleasure again, but meets a handsome Australian sheep rancher who tests this pledge.

Visit Our Website

For The Full Inventory
Of Quality Books:

Wings ePress, Inc

Quality trade paperbacks and downloads

in multiple formats,

in genres ranging from light romantic comedy to general fiction and horror.

Wings has something for every reader's taste.

Visit the website, then bookmark it.

We add new titles each month!

Wings ePress Inc.
3000 N. Rock Road
Newton, KS 67114

CPSIA information can be obtained
at www.ICGtesting.com
Printed in the USA
LVHW081926141219
640492LV00013B/260/P